CW00864665

CATS
OF THE RIVERLANDS

THE GOLDEN Statue

LISA FLAUM

ILLUSTRATONS BY CLAUDIA KOTZEN

To
Seth, Jonathan and Gabrielle.
May you never forget
who you really are.

CHAPTER ONE

Aloof but curious, Tikana lay camouflaged in one of the overhanging trees. She could scan the entire area from her perch high above Trade Point Wall. As soon as the shadows were long enough, trading would begin down below her. Trading was carefully controlled by the sentries and only domestic traders could appear at Trade Point Wall. On the other side lived the wild cats and their river fish. The sentries moved through the crowd, carefully checking the cats' trading bags. If a statue had been found, it would surely appear. Tikana had never cared for river fish, but seeing a real golden statue caught her in the chest. Had it really been found at last?

The sniffing crowd was already gathered up against the wall, while sentries hissed orders to move back. A fly interrupted her thoughts, and she batted it down with her paw. In the distance a darkening sky flashed and rumbled.

"And what would you be doing up here, just before trading begins?" meowed Buzz as he spotted Tikana from an adjacent perch.

Tikana's hair gave away her obvious fright, and she dug her claws deep into the bark, her eyes pinned to the far horizon.

"Wanting to trade, Princess?" he hissed, shaking his large trading bag and jumping onto her branch. Tikana's claws pulled white against her paws.

"Buzz, there isn't space for both of us!" she spat.

"Of course there is!" Buzz smiled, and he sat down right behind her. "You're just not used to hanging out with other cats! You really should try to be more social, you know. And by the way, you may not be visible from the ground, but you certainly are visible from over the wall. Wild cats don't enjoy being spied on."

Tikana hadn't thought about that, and a shiver ran down her spine. She scanned the neighbouring acacia trees on the other side of the wall for movement.

"Hoping to see a statue, perhaps?" continued Buzz as he breathed onto her back.

"Stop it!" snapped Tikana. "You're not scaring me. You're just irritating. ...BUUUZZZ!" cried Tikana as the branch tipped forward. She was trapped and precariously close to falling. A panicky feeling came over her as Buzz lowered his bag, tipping the branch further forwards.

"No, please!" exclaimed Tikana, her stapled claws threatening to tear from her skin.

"But I'd just like to show you my beautiful wind chime," mewed Buzz, opening his bag.

Tikana blinked as the metal tubes caught the setting sun. Sweet hypnotic vibrations poured out as Buzz unrolled them.

Down below, the crowd fell still and peered up into the trees. Tikana's golden-brown Abyssinian coat made her one with the branch in the dappled shade.

"Who's up there?" called a sentry.

A breeze caught the chimes a second time, increasing their singing.

"You know the penalty for illegal trading!" he shouted. "Show yourself or face banishment!"

Buzz silenced the tubes and wrapped them back in his bag. Behind Tikana, his tuxedo markings could not be seen from the ground. He slunk backwards in slow motion, and the branch once again steadied.

"Thanks, my darling,..." he whispered back to Tikana. Tikana's tail whipped from side to side, her whiskers sizzling.

"Like I don't know what you're up to," mewed Tikana, scanning the adjacent trees a second time. She may have been camouflaged a moment ago, but now, she was a sitting duck.

The skittish mob was once again a chorus of cat calls and hissing. Tikana was searched through by hungry eyes, some of the cats even heading for the base of the tree, trying to spot the mysterious chiming, until the unthinkable happened....

Drawn by the music, a curious wild cat leapt up onto the wall, back arched and eyes wide.

"We know there's a statue!" he hissed. The guards were on him in a flash. With clawing talons and guttural cries, he was wrestled down and flung back over the wall. The frenzied crowd stepped back. New excitement spiking their fur, they quite forgot about the mysterious noise up the tree.

Buzz seized the opportunity and disappeared deep into the darkening shadows, leaving Tikana without breath.

Movement in a tree on the other side of the wall caught her eye. The thin leaves revealed the shapes of three wildcats, their eyes and fangs flashing in her direction. Could they make the jump, branch to branch over the wall? Tikana's body quivered at the thought. Her shallow breathing was making her head spin, and she lowered her face between her front paws for a moment.

A rising wave of siren cat cries blew through the trees as storm clouds covered the sun.

"Trading is off," commanded the sentry in charge, his voice rising above the din. "All cats are to disperse immediately."

Danger shook the tree as another crack of thunder made Tikana look up. Waiting for movement, her stalkers prowled, closer still, edging their way out along the branches towards the wall. It was now or never. A strong gust of wind shook the tree, and Tikana eased backwards towards the thick of the trunk. Turning with a last look towards the acacia trees, she parachuted down, branches whizzing past her, leaves chasing her. She landed hard, sending a family of doves into the air.

Tikana sniffed back up into the dense branches at the leaping shadows, her heart pounding in her chest.

"And what are you doing here?" a gruff voice hissed from behind her.

Tikana turned into the air, swiping a front claw.

"Easy now," said the sentry, ducking from her attack. "You're very twitchy."

Tikana breathed a sigh of relief and bowed her head. "I'm sorry," she panted. "It's just the thunder, I guess." She glanced up into the tree.

"Best you be getting home now. There may be wild cats coming over the fence." He nodded in the direction of the houses.

Tikana raced over the grass and up the path. Dodging only at the odd crack of thunder, she ran until she was at her door.

"What are you running from?" mused Buzz, strewn across his neighbouring doormat.

"Six wildcat eyes, Buzz," panted Tikana. "Thanks to your greed and playing above the rules, I nearly got into serious trouble."

"What? No one could see you from the ground!" He sat up, curious.

"Not from the ground. From over the wall."

Buzz came closer and stroked his trading bag with his tail. "Sounds like I owe you a fish," Buzz purred. "Just the attention I needed."

"You're the last neighbour I would like owing me anything," she hissed as she shoved open her cat flap. "One day, Buzz," she meowed, "the boundaries will push back against you. I only hope you will survive them."

Buzz's heart skipped a beat at her words, and his ears shot back defensively.

"Who made up the trading rules anyway?" he called into the now closed cat flap. "Sentries think they're so high and mighty, guarding us traders..."

He swung his trading bag over his shoulder and headed back down the stairs. Tikana sat, heart racing, in her hallway, listening to Buzz's ranting becoming fainter.

CHAPTER TWO

Buzz sniffed the dark air and strained his whiskers. With his cat eyes he could usually see for miles at night, but heavy storm clouds hung low over the moon. There were no shadows, only blackness and the odd flash of lightning skipping over the grass and reflecting in the river. The thunder was getting louder and closer, and Buzz knew he would have to be quick. A swift jump from the tree, and his paws dusted the river sand below.

A crack lit up the sky, and there in front of him was the den: a large hole between two boulders. There was no sign of anyone, yet danger stroked his fur up the wrong way.

Buzz knew better than to make a deal with one of the wild cats, but his love for river fish drove him into extremely hazardous situations. Wildcat legends spoke of poisonous claws and jagged teeth, giants and speeds you could never escape from. Buzz held these stories at the back of his head somewhere, remembered from his childhood. Having actually seen and spoken to some of the wild cats, he knew there was some truth in the legends. They were not to be trusted. He would never take any of them on in a fight without losing his life.

But his stomach always seemed to be braver than his brain. Just the thought of River Fish Pie had him quickly purring. Or was it greed? Tikana's words churned in his chest. Selling it to the cats in the River Glades Estate was a highly lucrative business. They would never risk their lives to trade with wild cats without a sentry to negotiate. Besides, it was strictly forbidden.

Buzz had been offered six fish in exchange for his beautiful wind chime.

But now there was no sign of any traders and no smell of freshly caught river fish. Buzz put down his wind chime and buried it in the sand. He crept towards the entrance of the den. The howling wind boxed his ears, lifting grit into his eyes.

"Psst, Buzz," a voice came from above him.

Buzz jumped in fright and looked up. It was Asti, one of the wild she-cats. Buzz had traded with her a few weeks before.

"Get out of here Buzz! It's a trick. There is no..."

Asti's voice was caught in the wind, and she disappeared before Buzz understood what she was trying to say.

He turned to dig up the wind chime, but it was too late. Standing on top of the buried chimes was a giant wildcat. A flash of lightning lit his face for an instant, and Buzz recognized him. It was Jethro, the most evil wild cat at the river. Jethro loved to fight, and just one scratch from his claw could be deadly.

Buzz backed up slowly, only to feel a large paw pressing his tail into the dirt.

"And what do we have here?" hissed a gruff voice. Buzz recognized it as Jake, one of Jethro's best friends. Jake had killed many a cat. He too was a fighter, known by some as Death Blow Jake. Buzz knew that if he wanted to live, he must escape and run faster than legends!

Flinging a paw of river sand into Jake's face, he felt his tail being released. He made a flying leap into the bushes above him. The branches and thorns whizzed past his body as he dashed through the trees towards the estate. The perimeter lights beckoned him home, and with one last effort he flew through the tall grass and slipped between the palisades.

The soft grass of the complex garden soothed his paws as well as his heart. Heaving from the run, he stopped to catch his breath. Buzz swore and spat on the path. Turning back towards the fence, he saw four golden eyes flash before disappearing into the blackness. A trail of evil laugher echoed through the night.

The wild cats rarely entered the complex for fear of being captured and taken to the animal sanctuary. They loved their freedom and wild cat life. Legends at the river were often told of cages and cruelty at the hands of humans.

Buzz knew this and knew that he was safe. But at the back of his mind he also knew he had come far too close to death.

They could easily have followed him through the fence. Buzz wondered if he was at last becoming what his father had always feared, a law unto himself. Tikana's face also stared at him in disgust. He shivered and flicked his tail. "Ten lives left," he mumbled. It was his magic chant to banish fear and his father's words.

Buzz wanted his wind chime. In fact, he would have gone back for it the following night, but it was the quarter season assembly, and he never missed an important event. The wind chime would have to wait one more day.

CHAPTER THREE

right and full, the moon bathed the cats of the River Glades Estate in light. The assembled crowd made a sea of vibrant colours and shades. Domestic cats, all owned by the residents of the large housing estate.

Winding along a river, the estate was completely enclosed by a large palisade fence. In some places the fence was right up against the courtyard walls of some private gardens. A nasty electric fence on top of the walls and the palisade kept burglars out. The cats could easily slip between the palisades or under the electric wires on top of the walls, but only the Prince's sentries ever did. Most of the domestic cats were too afraid of what lay beyond their neat borders. Except for Buzz, of course.

The sentries were highly trained tomcats, forming a strict hierarchy. They guarded the complex from thieving wild cats looking for a fight, and each one kept tight control of his territory. The assemblies happened four times a year, kept in order by these toms.

A hum of excitement hung over the courtyard as the cats meowed and hissed. It was Magnum's turn to chair tonight's meeting. Looking out over the crowd, he caught the eye of his favourite blue Siamese she-cat. He puffed out his chest and hissed the meeting to order.

"Cats of the River Glades Estate," began Magnum, "I welcome you all on behalf of the prince."

There was a murmur through the crowd as everyone looked for Prince Tafari.

"Unfortunately, he is not able to join us in person tonight but has left me in charge."

The crowd sighed, disappointed. Prince Tafari was the most handsome tomcat on the property. Large and muscular, he was half Abyssinian and half African wild cat. He had pure royal blood on both sides, but to the cats of the River Glades, he was mostly a mystery. Although hardly ever seen, he knew everything that was happening on the estate.

The meeting continued. All sorts of issues were raised, from unruly Jack Russells to geese and of course the problem of trading fairly with the wild cats.

"And that brings us to the most important part of our meeting." Magnum was almost purring as he spoke. Things were going so well. "The introduction of all new cats."

He began to call out their names one by one as he sauntered proudly along the courtyard fence, quite unaware that flying off the balcony above him was a small ball of orange fluff.

On collision, Magnum was tossed from his perch into the bushes below.

There was a stunned silence as the crowd looked on. Covered with sticks and leaves, Magnum slowly emerged. A little dizzy, he tried to recover himself. He was bruised— not only his body, but also his pride. Turning to the shocked onlookers, he continued the ceremony.

"And the next newcomer to the estate is…"

But Magnum became aware that no one was listening to him. The cats had locked their gaze behind him. A ball of leaves and twigs and striped orange fur was staggering towards him.

Magnum raised his voice and tried again. "And the next newcomer to the estate is…"

But alas, it was no use. An older she-cat was striding towards the kitten, all ready to give him a good clean. Magnum quickly raised his paw to stop her and turned towards the intruder.

"Well, I suppose the next newcomer to the estate is you!" he said. "And you are…?"

The very dazed kitten looked up at Magnum and smiled. He was quite unaware of the seriousness of the ceremony and really too little to know how to behave in front of so many cats.

"The name is PC," said the kitten. "I sure am pleased to meet you!" He lifted up his paw to high-five Magnum.

Magnum didn't move a muscle, and PC kind of waved at him and then lowered his paw, grinning at the crowd.

"PC!" replied Magnum with a cough. "What sort of name is that?"

PC stopped smiling and backed off a few steps.

"What does it mean—personal computer?"

"I am not sure," answered PC softly, trying to smile again.

"Well," continued Magnum, rather enjoying his regained sense of power, "do speak up, pumpkin pie."

The crowd laughed, making PC feel a bit scared and embarrassed.

"Cat got your tongue?"

PC was as feisty as any tomcat twice his size, but now his ears cowered back, and his tail pressed between his legs. Tears began to well up in his eyes. The other cats roared with laughter—all except Tikana.

"That's enough," she exclaimed, her voice quietening the crowd. "He's only a kitten."

"Not the bleeding hearts club again!" grumbled Magnum, unaware at first of who was protesting.

"You have got to be kidding me!" he gasped as Tikana stepped forwards. "You have no authority to address me like that. Just because you're a golden Abyssinian doesn't mean you're above us mere cats! Acting like a princess doesn't make you one!"

"I was simply..."

"Simply interfering as usual," interrupted Magnum.

"Not true!" replied Tikana, immediately wishing she hadn't reacted to his comments. "I just don't think it's necessary to belittle a kitten when all he did was accidentally fall from a balcony!"

"Oh come on, Princess T," yelled Buzz. "We're just having a laugh!"

Tikana spun around, scanning the crowd for his whereabouts. "No, Buzz!" she called into the crowd. "Surely we're bigger than this. What will PC learn is right?"

"Here you go again," meowed Buzz loudly. "Next we'll all be getting a lecture on boundaries from Her Preachiness!"

Tikana's hair bristled. It was foolishness to speak up, but she could not tolerate bullying of any sort.

"Miss High and Mighty!" hissed some of the tabbies.

Voices and laughter came at her from all sides.

Tikana could feel herself breaking inside.

"Just ignore them, PC!" Her voice cracked, and she took a few steps backwards.

Magnum knew this could all end in a huge catfight and quickly looked for the other two sentries in charge. Scanning the crowd, he caught a glimpse of his beloved Siamese. She looked really upset by the whole incident.

"Damn Siamese cats," he mumbled. "Always so oversensitive!" But he wasn't about to lose her affection and quickly brought the meeting to order.

"I have decided," he began, "to bring tonight's meeting to an early close. However, as punishment for disrupting the meeting, I am assigning you, Tikana, as a guide for PC."

There was a snigger across the crowd.

"You will show this little naartjie the entire estate tomorrow, and make sure he doesn't come home without some knowledge of the rules! Meeting over!"

Glaring and hissing at Tikana as they passed, the cats quickly dispersed, becoming shadows in the night. Soon only PC and Tikana were left in the cold courtyard.

"Are you all right, little guy?" she asked.

PC nodded his head and looked towards his apartment.

"They are not all bad, PC. You'll make friends soon enough!" she added. Her mother had said the same to her, but it hadn't happened, and she had learnt to live without companionship.

"Well, I suppose I'll see you tomorrow," said Tikana, suddenly feeling bleak about her assignment—it was so far to walk and with the possibility of so much teasing and sniggering along the way. "Make sure you eat breakfast," she called out, skipping off down the stairs to her flat. "It's a long way for such a small kitten as you."

She was gone before PC even managed to say thank you or good-bye. All alone, he missed the comfort of his mother. He had just wanted to make friends and really hadn't meant to fall off the balcony.

At that moment, he felt himself being lifted up by a big hand. "Here you are, silly," said a voice. It was his owner, who was always kind and loving. "You're much too little to be down here by yourself," she said. "Come. Let's go inside for some nice warm milk."

CHAPTER FOUR

ikana sat perched on the edge of the fountain, her fur glistening and golden in the morning light. PC burst out of his cat flap and ran towards her. Flying up onto the fountain wall, he almost slipped into the water below.

"Careful now," gasped Tikana, steadying him with her paw. She jumped off the wall, and PC followed.

The two began their journey in silence, unsure of each other. Tikana hoped that no one would see them carrying out this punishment. Shame smeared over her.

It wasn't long before they came upon a very large Persian with a cream moustache. Tikana's heart sank, and she tried to speed up her pace, hoping that perhaps he wouldn't even notice them.

But PC had never seen a cat like this before and slowed down until he almost tripped over his own feet. His eyes were large with excitement. The Persian had so much fur he was as round as a ball. In fact, PC wasn't sure if he had legs at all and immediately moved towards him to get a closer look. He was quite unaware of Tikana's efforts to hurry past.

The fur on the Persian's back rose, making him even bigger and fluffier than before, and PC froze.

"Get off my path!" he hissed.

Suddenly PC's legs seemed stuck to the ground, and he couldn't move.

Coming closer, the Persian repeated himself. He hissed and moved well within striking distance, his tail swishing the leaves on the bricks.

"PC!"

Moved by Tikana's urgent call, PC took a flying leap sideways off the path, just missing a swipe from a large, fluffy paw.

"Follow me," instructed Tikana, and she raced down the side of a cottage with PC close behind her. Panting, they came to a stop under a large paper bark tree.

"Well," said Tikana when she had caught her breath, "that was close. Shall we continue?"

PC was motionless.

"Are you all right?" asked Tikana, feeling very big next to her companion. "That oversized fluff ball is just a cranky old tomcat! Don't let him scare you. Now sniff the air. Cats must always be aware of all the smells in the area; that way you can tell if there is danger approaching. And..." she said with a wry smile on her face, "whatever you have done wrong, always try to make it look like the dog did it!"

She turned towards PC, smiling. He was unfrozen and had spotted a bright orange butterfly. Balancing up on his hind legs, he was trying to catch it.

What fun! What a game!

Tikana was not amused. She crouched low, then lifted into the air and pounced onto PC, pinning him to the ground.

"PC," she said sternly, "you must stay with me and listen. It can be very dangerous out here!"

"I'll try," said PC. "It's just that there are so many new and exciting things to see I can't help myself. I never dreamt of seeing a cat so fat his legs were missing or a tiny bird with orange wings!"

Tikana smiled again. "That tiny bird is a butterfly," she said. Then, quickly changing her tone, she looked at PC in earnest. "There are dogs and geese and snakes and sometimes even wild cats."

PC's eyes glistened. "I'll scratch any Jack Russell through with my claw and rip the feathers from a goose!" He punched the air as he spoke. "And the wild cats, are they giants with claws like knives and teeth like nails?" His eyes sparkled with adventure.

"No," replied Tikana, sighing. She lowered his fisted paw to the ground. "But they can all be unpredictable."

Although Tikana had never actually seen a wild cat up close, she knew what they smelt like. She had caught glimpses of them through the fence and heard descriptions, especially from Buzz. She knew he always exaggerated everything, but his accounts had nevertheless made her quite apprehensive.

The morning passed quickly, and by midday PC was starting to tire. His legs were moving in slow motion, and Tikana was sure he had stopped listening. A shortcut home would be the best option.

Lost in her own thoughts after PC's endless questions, Tikana didn't notice that they were coming into an enclosed courtyard, surrounded by a wall and overhanging trees.

She stopped dead in her tracks, the hair on her back standing straight up.

"What's wrong, Tikana?" asked PC.

"Hush," she answered quickly. "Just back up slowly. I don't think we have been spotted."

PC felt the hair on his back stand up too, only he didn't know why. He felt a kind of excitement and fear rush down his spine, and then he became aware of an unfamiliar smell. He sniffed the air.

"What you are smelling," whispered Tikana as they backed up together, "is river fish. At my signal, turn and run. Now!"

Like lightning, the two cats dashed out of the courtyard around the corner and up one of the overhanging trees.

They held still in the branches and caught their breath. Down below them, a dark figure stepped into the sunlight. She was carrying a small brown bag.

Tikana crept close to PC. "Whatever you do, don't make a sound," she whispered. "As luck has it, the wind is blowing towards us, and they shouldn't smell us at all."

PC watched wide-eyed as three giant cats landed softly on the paving. They had been in the trees on the other side of the courtyard.

"Wild cats!" whispered Tikana. "They live at the river on the other side of that wall."

Tikana could feel her thumping chest and she moved closer to PC.

CHAPTER FIVE

The three wild cats hissed as they spoke.

"You'll get the fish when we're satisfied! Now let the cat out of the bag!" Jethro's eyes flashed green and gold as he spoke.

"So hand it over, pussycat," interrupted the large grey cat next to Jethro—clearly a runaway. He spat as he spoke through his toothless mouth, his icy blue eyes fixed on the bag. "You can trust us!"

The cat with the bag stepped forward into the sunlight. Tikana gasped as she recognized her. It was a river trader, a distant relative, but nobody knew or suspected, as they looked so different. Tikana, with her golden fur and beautiful white markings, was nothing like her cousin, who was covered in a soft, creamy fluff from head to toe.

"I want ten fish for this," she said, her voice quivering a bit. "What I have here is worth more than six, and you know that!"

The third cat rose up like a giant. "Just show us the statue!" he sneered, his ears twitching.

"Silence Jake! I will handle this trade myself." Jethro's piercing voice echoed around the courtyard. Jake, the third cat, slunk back.

Cautiously the river trader opened the bag and lifted out its contents.

Tikana and PC were blinded at first as they peered down. A small golden statue, glittering in her paws, had caught the sunlight.

Jethro moved forward, casting a shadow, and the figure was clear for all to see. The wild cats hissed and purred with delight, their tails swishing from side to side.

In the trees above them, PC and Tikana stared in silent amazement. The statue was of a proud, sitting cat, most certainly royal.

"It's not a myth!" gasped Tikana in a whisper. "And it's so beautiful."

"But Tikana," gulped PC audibly, "that statue is you!"

The cats in the courtyard scanned the trees above them. Tikana knew they had been overheard. It would only be a matter of seconds before they were spotted.

"We've got to get out of here," said Tikana, startled, "and the only way of escape is onto that roof over there." PC followed her eyes to the roof about a metre from the branch they were on.

"But we can't go all the way down and up the stairs," pleaded PC. "We'll be caught!"

"No," said Tikana firmly. "We're going to have to jump! I'll go first. Just follow my footing."

Caught in terror, PC could not move. His heart was beating so fast he wondered if it could actually fall out.

In a second Tikana had cleared the branches and was leaping for the thatch. PC followed, jumping with all his might onto the roof. But never having landed on thatch before, he immediately started sliding.

"Tikana! Help me!" he called.

Quick as a flash, Tikana grabbed his paw, but the thatch was too slippery, and PC was too heavy.

"Land on the windowsill," she gasped as PC disappeared from view.

PC landed with a thud, not on the windowsill, but right inside someone's lounge.

He jumped to his feet and leapt up towards the open window. It was too late. The three wild cats were already there, waiting to catch him.

Jethro placed his paw firmly on PC's tail, the tip of his claw piercing through his flesh.

"And what do we have here?" spat Jethro. "A little spy!"

"There is no living for spies," hissed Jake, the scar on his ear twitching again as he spoke.

"Prepare to die, fuzzball," he said as he grabbed PC by the scruff of his neck.

PC couldn't move or speak; in fact, he was struggling to breathe.

Even bigger up close, the wild cats smelt of sweat and dried blood, their claws thick with rotting flesh and dark soil. They were terrifying.

"Wait... not here, Jake," hissed Jethro. He turned to PC and snarled, "You're coming with us." Jethro sharpened his talons on the windowsill. "We wouldn't want you talking now would we?"

Jake tightened the skin around PC's neck, then flung him at Jethro, who dragged him off the windowsill, his fangs gripping the fur on PC's back.

CHAPTER SIX

ikana crouched behind a wind vane. She watched as the wild cats disappeared over the wall, PC firmly in tow. What should she do now? No one would believe her. They probably wouldn't even listen to her if she asked for help.

The weather vane above her turned its back on Tikana, and a gust of wind almost swept her off the roof. A storm was approaching; the distant rain reached Tikana's nostrils, and the trees started to dance wildly. Tikana had never felt so alone. Her mother's face flashed before her. She hadn't thought about her mother for months.

Almost audibly, she could hear a lullaby her mother sang to her, caught in the wind. "Hush, little princess. Close your eyes…" She had the sweetest voice, and for a moment, Tikana was deeply comforted.

It seemed strange that she should think of her now. And then it dawned on her: the statue! The little golden statue that the wild cats stole wasn't of her, but of her mother. Seeing it must have brought her mother to mind, and now, all alone and in trouble, Tikana needed her desperately. She knew it was a useless thought, as her mother had left the complex shortly after she had been sold. She had gone with her owners to a new house up the river.

The singing stopped, and Tikana put her face to the wind. She strained to hear the soothing voice again. Then, quite unexpectedly, she heard with her heart, the words that her mother had said before she left—words that lingered deep inside her.

"Tikana, be strong now. Know that you are a princess among cats. You will not always be honoured as a princess should, and many will be jealous of you. But nobility, although it is a birth right, can be every cat's inheritance. Noble character is far more powerful than any proof."

She felt the words hit her stomach as she understood them for the first time. They were an invitation to be someone, to belong.

Tikana thought again about the statue and took a flying leap for the wall. She had never gone down to the river, and although her mind was crying out NO, her heart moved her body. She would have to go and try to rescue PC.

CHAPTER SEVEN

Buzz was in a bad mood. He had missed a night of adventure, and now a storm was coming. A flooded river would be sure to wash his wind chime away. He had to be quick. Preferring to go to the river under the cover of darkness, Buzz crossed his claws that the wild cats near the den would be asleep.

Crouching to jump over the wall, Buzz noticed a small brown bag lying in the courtyard. He had seen it before and recognized it as belonging to one of the river traders. He picked it up and sniffed it. Empty. Buzz knew that something was wrong.

"Buzz, quickly, over here," whispered a voice from behind a nearby doorway. He followed the voice under the archway.

"You," said Buzz, as his eyes adjusted to the shadows. "What's happened?"

The river trader was furious.

"I was tricked," she snarled. "I should have known not to trust those half breeds!"

Buzz didn't really like her. She gave the river traders a bad name. She often kept fish for herself and would charge the cats way too much for her trading services.

But for some reason Buzz felt sorry for her today.

"Look," she said, pointing to her front paw. There was a large scratch, red with dried blood. "Jake did this as he snatched my trade!" she snapped. "And I got nothing in return. We were about to do a deal when Jethro started yelling about spies. Jake snatched the goods, and they headed up those stairs."

Buzz listened attentively, his whiskers stiffening.

"It gets worse," she continued. "When they came back down, they had a kitten with them, an orange stripy one. Why would the wild cats want a domestic kitten?"

Buzz took in her every word, and his whiskers started to twitch with excitement.

"What did you have in that bag?" he asked.

"Oh, just something I found," she said, trying to sound casual.

Buzz spoke sternly. "Whatever it is, it must be very valuable. Wild cats don't just go around kidnapping spies."

He leaped onto the wall.

"Where are you going?" she whined, still feeling sorry for herself.

"To fetch Tafari," said Buzz. "It's PC's only hope."

"Who's PC?" she exclaimed, trying to catch up with Buzz. But she couldn't hear his answers, as the wind was chasing them, and Buzz was already over the wall.

CHAPTER EIGHT

Jake breathed onto the statue, making it mist up for a few seconds, and then turned towards Jethro.

"Quite like this piece of gold, Jethro. You got a plan to make us rich?" His eyes narrowed, and he flexed his leg muscles.

"The statue is mine," interrupted Jethro, snatching it from Jake. Jethro's tail swished in anger, and he arched his back. "Don't even try to double cross me, Jake. The statue belongs to me, and you know that."

From a dark corner of the den, PC was listening. He was hungry and tired and frightened out of his wits. But curiosity was lurking in his mind—oh to see that statue again!

Jake and Jethro started to hiss and circle each other.

A voice came from the darkness on the other side of the den. "If you two will calm down, I have a plan in which we can all have part of the statue. I propose we melt it down and then divide the gold into three parts, one for each of us."

It was the third wild cat, the one with the piercing blue eyes.

Choking and spitting, Jethro held up the statue. "This little statue is not just a piece of gold," he bawled. "It is the proof of nobility—my nobility! Statues like this only belong to royalty and are passed down from one generation to the next. Don't you see, my friends?" he continued. "This is not just a trade but my ticket back to power and privileges."

Proof of nobility? Jethro's words echoed in PC's head. Was Tikana a real princess?

Jethro interrupted his thoughts with a sudden roar. "Fetch me the kitten!" He grew taller and larger as he spoke. The other two cats looked on in amazement as their leader transformed before their eyes.

Jake was quick to bring PC to the entrance of the den.

"No one shall take this power away from me!" roared Jethro. "From this day forth, I am the Prince of the Wild Cats. Jake, take this miniature spy and drown him forthwith in the river."

Panic seared through PC's little body. He had caught a glimpse of the river as they had entered the den. It was much too deep for him and the current too strong. He would never make it.

"Help! Help me, somebody!" cried PC. Wrestling and scratching at his ropes, he hissed like mad.

"Shut your mouth!" snarled Jake, smothering his cries with a hard-pressed paw.

CHAPTER NINE

With a soft puff, Tikana dusted the river sand below the forbidden wall and sniffed the air. All the smells were unfamiliar and made the hair on her back stand up. Ahead of her were a trail, paw marks, and scuffed sand, obviously where they had dragged PC. She felt that pain in her chest again.

"And who are you?" a soft voice came from behind her, making her whole body jerk with fright. She swung around. Nothing. She could only see her footprints.

Tikana's very breath became loud. Was she starting to hear things? She slunk forwards.

"Who are you, stranger?" whispered the voice again.

Tikana's chest felt squeezed.

"I said, who are you?"

Tikana refused to turn around. A leaf floated down, just missing her whiskers, and she looked up. There was the source of the voice, high up in the trees above her.

"Don't be afraid. I'm Asti, and I've never seen you here before. Are you wanting to trade?" Her voice was soothing, almost hypnotic, and Tikana felt herself being drawn up into the branches.

A gust of wind caught Tikana in the face. She blinked to get the sand out of her eyes. When her sight returned, Asti was standing right in front of her. She was not black or brown but a deep midnight blue colour, with beautiful Siamese eyes.

"Silence and secrets?" Asti purred.

Tikana was unsure. Could she trust this cat. Could any of the wild cats be trusted? She certainly was beautiful—not like any of the wild cats in Buzz's stories. Her coat was glistening, and her words were pronounced with confidence and elegance.

"Well, are you looking for something, dear one?" Asti tried again, all the while staring at her with a deep questioning look, as though she was remembering someone.

Tikana felt she had no choice.

"Y-y-yes," she stuttered. "I've lost my friend. He was taken——kidnapped by three big wild cats, and I am here to try to find him."

Asti flew up into the tree, beckoning Tikana to go with her. "No time must be wasted," said Asti, asking no further questions. "Follow me, and don't speak unless I ask you a question."

CHAPTER TEN

The trees whizzed past their ears as the two cats sped through the branches, dropping a trail of leaves behind them. A strong wind was coming up, and the approaching storm made the branches sway furiously. Tikana had never run at this pace through trees and was relieved when they finally came to a stop.

"There," gasped Asti, pointing down between the branches. "There is the den, and there is your friend!"

Tikana looked down just in time to see Jake lift PC high up into the air above the river.

"No!" exclaimed Tikana, losing her balance and taking Asti with her. Crashing down through the branches they landed with a thud.

Jake swung around. Asti turned to flee, but her tail was caught in something sharp, something half buried in the sand. Jake slowly lowered PC back onto the riverbank. He had a sort of puzzled look on his face and just kept staring at Tikana, almost as if he had seen her somewhere before.

Then he turned his attention towards Asti, his eyes cold and hard. He dragged PC along with him till he was right up close to her. "What the hell are you doing here?" he spat. "Want to finish what we started all those years ago?"

With that he released one claw and lightly scraped it under her chin. She flinched for a second and then looked him straight in the eyes.

Tikana held her breath. She thought Asti was sure to cry at any minute, but she was calm and still like a statue, her tail caught and obviously hurting.

"I'm not scared of you, Jake," she hissed. "Even at the river there are rules, and you know that. When Tafari hears about this, you'll pay!"

Tikana's head was racing. Was Tafari also Prince of the River Lands? Tikana had only seen him once before, when she was very young, and then it had only been for a second.

She had been playing around the fountain by herself when the whole complex fell still. There was no wind, and the fountain itself stopped. As she gazed at herself in the glass-like water, a large figure joined her. She was so mesmerized by his reflection that she wondered afterwards whether she had been dreaming. His markings were an unusual brown colour on his creamy golden body, turning almost black on his broad, handsome face and tattooing the rims of his pale green eyes. His legs were striped, and a dark line ran down his spine, colouring the tip of his tail in chocolate. He was all muscle under his glistening coat. Their eyes had met in the water for a second until he leaned down to drink. The ripples merged their reflections. He was gone before she could even look up.

Tikana's thoughts were broken by a loud crack of thunder, and all the cats crouched low.

"Bowing thus before me, are you?" a new voice boomed from the entrance to the den. It was Jethro. Larger than anyone had ever seen him, he had a hungry look of power in his eyes and was quite transformed. He looked meaner than ever, like an evil prince. All the cats shivered.

Jethro turned his attention to Jake. "Can't you do anything properly? This little orange fluff ball should be deceased by now. Instead he has guests!"

Large drops of rain started to fall, shooting dust clouds into the air.

"Get into the den, all of you!" Jethro ordered. They were quick to obey, even Asti, yanking her tail free and leaving a huge tuft of fur on the metal object.

CHAPTER ELEVEN

Asti had never been inside their den before, and the dim light made her feel closed in. The air was stale and smelt of rotting wood. It was filthy and full of half-chewed bird bones and broken furniture.

Her front paws started to quiver, and she quickly tucked them under her chest. Never having seen Jethro like this, Asti felt fear rising. She kept trying to remind herself of Prince Tafari and knew he would come to their rescue—that is, if he knew that they were in trouble.

PC was feeling warmed by Tikana's presence, and his violent shaking slowed down. The three of them crouched in the flickering candlelight of the den.

"Trust you to have friends from over the fence," snarled Jake at Asti. "You should have thought more carefully before befriending my enemies." He lowered his voice to a whisper. "Go on then. Tell Jake here who she is." He stared at Tikana, his eyes roaming over her sleek golden body.

"I don't know their names," answered Asti. "I only know that you are holding them here against their wishes, and that is against the law!"

"Law!" shrieked Jethro. "Whose law? I am now Prince of the River, and I make up the rules!"

"Oh no, you don't!" exclaimed Asti, anger overtaking her fear. "Tafari is Prince of the River! What you are speaking is treason!"

Jethro swung a paw at her, but Asti was far quicker than most cats and managed to duck. Embarrassed by his poor action, he immediately ordered Jake to tie her up.

"And bring forth those two spies," he ordered.

Not wanting to be dragged, Tikana stepped forward. In the torchlight, she looked pure gold, her fur catching the yellow light, and her white markings shining. Even Asti held her breath as Tikana came forward, and she realized then who Tikana must be. Jethro's ears pinned back, and for a few seconds he seemed to shrink down to his normal size. His beloved statue had come to life, showing him up as a thief. Where had she been all these years?

It was Jake who broke his trance. Sniffing the air, he hissed, and they all smelt it at once. Domestic cats, right outside the den.

CHAPTER TWELVE

afari had been difficult to track down, and even now Buzz couldn't keep up with him. He had reacted immediately to the report and disappeared over the wall. Buzz found the way tough, as the storm was making everything wet and slippery, and the wind made the branches unstable. He couldn't see Tafari anywhere and thought it best to try the den first. Buzz also thought it might be a chance for him to retrieve his chimes.

Creeping up to the den through the trees, Buzz could see the tip of his wind chime sticking up through the sand. Something was caught on it. He strained his eyes to try and make out what it was. If only he could get closer. In a flash he was on the ground.

Digging around his chimes in double time, he lifted them from the sand, and rolled them together. With a firm grip on them, he dashed back up a tree.

"Are you mad?" cried a voice in his head. "Is trading all you care about? You could have blown your cover with that stupid wind chime!"

"Quiet," said Buzz, dusting it off and inspecting the tip. A cat's tail fur and fresh blood were caught in the metal hook. Buzz recognized it at once as Asti's.

"There's big trouble up ahead," Buzz mumbled and looked around for Tafari.

At that moment Jake appeared at the entrance to the den. He sniffed the air a couple of times and strained his eyes in Buzz's direction. Buzz was downwind and sure he wouldn't be spotted, he moved to adjust his footing. Without thinking, he let go of the chimes with his left paw. A beautiful sound poured out of them, and their now lopsided weight, pulled him rather clumsily down to the ground.

Jake was onto him before Buzz had even landed.

Buzz swore under his breath. Jake kept a distance, however, wanting to stay near the entrance to the den, his eyes fixed on Buzz.

"There is no trading here tonight," shouted Jake through the wind, clearly irritated. "What are you doing here? Keen for another chase?"

"I'm here on other business," said Buzz. Jake's obvious need to stay close to the den gave Buzz courage. "A trade may be necessary. Seen any cats around here lately?"

Jake's lip twitched, and he glanced back towards the den. "Get out of here, moron!" he spat at Buzz. "There are hundreds of wild cats at the river. Of course I have seen cats around here. Are you stupid or something?"

"I'm looking for Asti," came Buzz's quick reply. He was unmoved by Jake.

"That witch!" sneered Jake. He looked at the ground momentarily and then straight at Buzz. "No. Why? What do you want with her—a spell?" An evil snigger formed on his lips. "Asti hasn't been seen for weeks!" he hissed. Then he paused and mumbled, "She may, in fact, never be seen again." He wiped the saliva from his whiskers.

"What did you say?" questioned Buzz forcefully, thinking he had heard Jake's mumbling.

Buzz knew he was lying, and he had the fur to prove it. "I know the truth," shouted Buzz, gaining courage. "You're nothing but a kidnapping thief!"

Spitting on the ground, Jake moved closer to Buzz. "That statue is ours now! Ours! Do you hear me?"

Buzz was speechless. Thoughts were racing through his mind. A statue! No, it couldn't be—not the missing statue!

Jake suddenly realized from the look on Buzz's face that he knew nothing of their acquisition of the statue. A deep laugh rose up from Jake, almost frightened and out of control. Then as quickly as the laughing started, it stopped, and Jake took a step towards Buzz.

"What we have is ours and is none of your business!" he yelled.

He said this so loudly that everyone in the den heard him, and Jethro felt it was time to investigate for himself.

Jethro's newfound power made him fearless, and with his other crony guarding the spies, he felt he could conquer the world.

"Well, well, well," began Jethro, exiting the den and striding up to the cats. "Jake, you haven't forgotten that the statue is mine, not ours?"

Jake hissed, his whole body taut with rage. Jethro pushed him aside and moved towards Buzz.

"What do you want? Trading is not for hours yet, and besides, by then I shall be Prince of the River and shortly after that, Prince of the River Glades Estate! You, little Buzzbee, will be my subject, and what is yours shall become mine. Without a trade! I have a statue—a real one. It's mine, and its power is mine!" he roared.

Rising once again, quite beyond his usual size to an enormous height, he towered above Buzz. There would be no way out for him now unless he ran for it. But with the rain and the wet branches, he would never make the fence before being taken down.

"In the meantime," continued Jethro, "you are on my land, and you will do as I command! One false move, and I'll strike you a deadly blow with my claw. Got it?"

Buzz was fuming inside and feeling very humiliated. He was a big cat and not afraid of anything except losing his reputation with the cats in the River Glades Estate. He was sure PC was in the den, and possibly Asti too. He must try to rescue them. He looked around for Tafari. There was no sign of him. Mustering up all his courage, he sat up and looked Jethro straight in the eye.

"Until you have won the River Lands fair and square, statue or no statue, you have a kitten in that den that you are holding against his wishes. Even you know that goes against every rule of the land, Jethro. Now I'll promise to keep it quiet if you hand him over to me."

Buzz held up the wind chimes. Moved by the breeze, their music was so beautiful, almost hypnotic. Jethro looked caught for a moment, as though a deep internal wrestle was going on. Then his face hardened, and he whispered into Jake's ear. Slinking backwards, Jake vanished into the den. Only moments later a frightened, quivering ball of orange fluff appeared at the entrance, Jake's claw holding him behind the ear.

"It's all right, PC," called Buzz reassuringly. "We'll get you away from these thieves. Here, Jethro. You can have the wind chime." He lifted it up and came closer to the cave. "Pass me the kitten, and I'll toss you the chimes."

"No!" snarled Jethro. "You pass me the chimes first, or the deal is off!"

Buzz hesitated. He had been tricked by the river cats before. But without Tafari, it was all he could do to save PC's life.

"All right," yelled Buzz. "Here. Catch!"

At that moment there was a cry from inside the cave. It was Asti trying to warn Buzz. It was too late; Buzz had already tossed them high up in the air towards the entrance of the den.

Dancing through the air to their own music, the chimes bounced across the sand before being silenced by four large, creamy, golden paws. Tafari stood absolutely still, balancing on the metal tubes, his muscles flexed, his eyes fixed on Jethro.

His presence made all the cats crouch low. Even Jethro shrank back to his normal size for a few moments.

"And who invited you?" snarled Jethro, quickly getting in the first word. "You are no longer Prince. I am! You are now my subject, and you must obey me!" As he spoke he grew large again, almost as big as Tafari.

Tafari didn't blink, his eyes continuing to blaze into Jethro. Time stood still.

"You are not a prince and never will be. You don't understand what it means to be royal. You never have."

With that, Jethro laughed long and loud, an evil, piercing laugh. "Bring me that statue!" he called into the den.

"What statue?" Tafari snapped, looking at Buzz for part of the story he had forgotten to tell him.

Grabbing his statue from the stray, Jethro laughed again and held the golden figure right up against Tafari's face.

Silence held everything still as the cats waited for his response. Even Asti and Tikana had made their way to the entrance of the den now that they were no longer guarded. Tafari lifted his paw and quite calmly moved Jethro's arm away from his face.

It was then that he first caught a glimpse of Tikana. Transfixed for a moment, he stared at her, a puzzled look coming over his face. She looked up and was caught in his gaze for an instant. He looked at the statue and then back at her. Tikana cast down her eyes.

It was PC's frightened cry that broke the silence. Jake's claw was digging into the side of his neck, tightening with every wriggle. PC's cries started to turn into frantic gagging moans.

"Quiet!" boomed Jethro swiping PC out of Jake's grip and sending him flying towards the river. Coughing, PC tried to get his breath back. A deadly torrent roared below him, its waters rising rapidly. The bank was wet and slippery, and PC started to slide down towards the river.

CHAPTER THIRTEEN

Buzz immediately tried to make a move towards PC but was grabbed by an angry Jake. He was furious with Jethro for removing his captive.

"Oh no, you don't!" he snarled. "That little spy should have died long ago!" And he threw Buzz to the ground. Jake spat at him, swinging a paw dangerously close to his left eye. Buzz crouched low and retreated.

"This statue," continued Jethro, quite unmoved by PC's plight, "is my proof of nobility, the proof that I am now Prince of the River Lands!"

"You fool!" said Tafari under his breath before launching himself on top of Jethro, digging his claws into his skin. The two cats rolled around and around in the mud, making it very difficult for the other cats to see what was happening. Lightning fast claws ripped through each other's fur. On and on they fought, parting only now and again to regain their position, both moving closer and closer to the river.

Meanwhile, PC continued to slip down the bank, his tiny claws unable to grip onto anything. It was Tikana who made a move to help him.

Unguarded, she slipped out of the den and made her way towards the river. PC had by now slipped out of sight.

"PC!" she screamed, trying to make herself heard above the roar of the river and the fighting cats. But he couldn't hear her. Again and again she called for him until he happened to look up and see her.

"I'll lower down this branch," she instructed. "Just hold it tight, and don't let go!"

He couldn't hear her, but when he saw the branch, he immediately grabbed onto it with all his might. She gripped it in her teeth and started to move backwards. Suddenly there was a jarring in her mouth, and the branch became very heavy. Tikana was pulled towards the river. PC had been knocked down by a new flood of water and was completely under the torrent. She strained with all her might and tried to pull him up, but the water was too deep, the current too strong.

Despairing, she closed her eyes and tried again.

The pain in her teeth eased as all of a sudden the branch became lighter.

"Oh no!" she gasped as she opened her eyes, expecting to see PC floating down the river. But all she could see was black and white fur. Buzz had managed to sneak to her side as the fight distracted the other cats. He pulled the branch with all his might, and together they watched as PC emerged from the river. Getting him up the bank was easy after that.

Out of breath, they stared at PC. He was a tiny dark orange ball, lying so still they didn't know whether or not to touch him.

"Do you think he's dead?" whispered Tikana. She had never seen a dead cat but started to feel a shiver go up her spine and a lame feeling come over her body. Her heart felt like it was being squeezed, and she struggled to breathe.

"Not definitely," answered Buzz, quickly patting and shaking PC.

There was no response.

CHAPTER FOURTEEN

J ethro realized that he was getting further away from his statue and began to manoeuvre the fight back towards it. He knew he must remain close to it in order to keep up his courage, and besides, he didn't want any of the other cats to get it.

As the statue came within reach, Jethro leaped for it, only to be pinned down immediately by Tafari. The statue slipped away and started to roll down the bank. A terror seized Jethro as he watched it plop into the river, sinking down under the current into the darkness below. As his nobility disappeared from view, he felt his pride burn. With one last ounce of strength, he managed to roll Tafari over, sinking his teeth into Tafari's neck. The force of the bite sent him rolling further until both cats were caught in a deadly slide. Tikana and Buzz gasped as they watched them disappear into the torrent below. Asti rushed to the edge of the bank, and a silence fell once again. They looked on in disbelief. There was no sign of either of the cats.

CHAPTER FIFTEEN

Turning back to PC, Buzz bashed his paw down hard on his chest. Tikana gasped and started crying. He did it a second time as the cats huddled around.

"I think it's too late, Tikana," whispered Buzz. Everyone crouched down around PC's little body, a tradition amongst the cats of the River Glades when another cat was passing on to the spaces between the stars. Tikana was now sobbing, her tears falling on PC's face. One tear rolled down inside his mouth.

Suddenly there was movement. PC coughed and then opened his eyes. Everyone jumped up and gazed on in disbelief.

"Will you take me home now?" he whispered, a little dazed and confused.

"Hush now," answered Tikana, laughing and purring at the same time. She didn't want to tell him about the fight and make him more frightened. She lay down next to him and started to dry him with her tongue, trying to keep him warm.

"Quickly, to the Silent Pools, everyone," commanded Buzz, realizing as he spoke that neither Tikana nor PC would have any idea where or what the Silent Pools were.

"Go. Hurry," urged Asti. "I'll look after Tikana and PC and bring them to Willow Tree Point."

Buzz grabbed his wind chime and sped off through the trees.

Jake and his sidekick had already disappeared through the bushes on the other side of the den.

"Cowards!" cried Asti after them, but her words were drowned out by the roar of the river, which was continuing to rise—and fast! Asti knew that the Silent Pools would soon become a death trap of whirling water and that it was the last safe point of rescue before Storm Water Falls.

She turned towards Tikana and, with an extended paw, lowered her eyes and whispered, "Your Majesty…"

Her words were caught by emotion. The rising of something so deep, like what you feel when you've had a dream and all of a sudden you're in your dream, and the feelings rush back, but it's daytime.

Tikana glanced at PC, embarrassed by the gesture. But it wasn't the same mocking "Princess" she had heard all her life. The one that had stifled and broken her; but it was a door opening to fresh air. PC had no idea what "Your Majesty" meant, but he smiled up at her, his rescuer and protector, his eyes quite adoring.

"Lead the way, Asti," she said at last. "We are in your hands."

CHAPTER SIXTEEN

uzz was quick to fly through the treetops. The only hope for Tafari would be if Buzz could get to the pools before him. Although the rain had stopped, there was still quite a wind, and the trees were very unstable. It was a race against time.

As Buzz reached the pools, he could hear Storm Water Falls roaring up ahead. Below him, the rapidly rising pools were still quiet. Buzz sped up an overhanging willow tree, his wind chime safely clutched in his mouth. The willow trees at the silent pools were old and broad, their thin branches stirring and stroking the water. Buzz gathered as many branches as he could between his paws and slid down until he was close enough for someone to use him as a lifesaver.

It seemed like minutes that he held on, all the time wondering if he was too late. A large gush of water filled the first pool above where he was hanging and then spilled over into the second underneath him. It filled so quickly that his tail and chimes were submerged, and Buzz climbed a bit higher. Then out of nowhere, he glimpsed a dark shadow under the water.

It rounded the corner into the first pool and then quick as a flash into the second. Buzz called out at the top of his voice, "Over here!"

He could not make out who it was at first, and a flood of relief came over him when he saw the familiar shape of Tafari, his muscular body carefully edging its way towards Buzz. He was ready to grab the wind chime. Suddenly a gust of wind moved Buzz over, and as Tafari reached out, it was too far. He would have to avoid the current that would sweep him into the third pool and swirl back towards Buzz. Buzz lowered himself again, lending more of his tail and clutching his wind chimes with his back legs, in case the branch moved again.

In a flash, Tafari was back in the whirlpool, and he lifted his body right up, beyond the chimes. Buzz felt an enormous weight grip him, and for a moment both cats were under the water. The branches rose with the momentum, and the cats gasped for air. Tafari dug his claws into Buzz before heaving himself up and over onto the branch above. The willow swung wildly.

Steadying himself, Tafari turned and offered Buzz his paw, gripping the thickest part of the branches with his back legs. As Buzz lifted his paw, fastening it steadily in Tafari's, the branches once again seemed weighed down, and before Buzz realized what was happening, a sharp pain filled his tail. He let go of Tafari and kicked with his back legs, his wind chimes falling deep into the pool. He felt a set of teeth grip his leg and sharp claws fasten around his waist.

It was Jethro.

Jethro swung his body weight, setting the branches in a wild swing, all the time biting and climbing up Buzz. Tafari edged backwards and used the movement of the branches to create an even stronger swing.

Buzz looked up and saw Tafari motion to him with his eyes. On the next swing, the branches would be just over the rocks, and if Buzz could get free of Jethro's grip, he could jump to safety. Unaware of their plan, Jethro continued to use Buzz as a climbing frame. The branches went into a rapid spin, slowing him down and making his climb difficult.

Buzz counted slowly in his mind, getting ready to jump. The spinning was making him feel disoriented and sick. Three, four, five, it was time…Buzz was free and launched in the direction of the rocks. He landed with a thud, half of his body submerged under the water. Using every last inch of energy, he pulled himself to safety, closed his eyes, and lost consciousness.

CHAPTER SEVENTEEN

Asti, Tikana, and PC made their way to Willow Tree Point. They moved slowly from branch to branch, Tikana helping PC when she saw he was fading. PC was starving and longed again for the warmth and comfort of his owner's flat. When at last Asti turned and said, "There it is!" all three cats were filled with energy to make the last few jumps onto the grassy bank. It was circular and completely surrounded by willow trees. It sloped up on one side where there was a flat rock, perfect for standing on and looking out over the area.

"This is where the wild cats meet," said Asti.

"How many wild cats are there?" asked Tikana. She didn't want to meet any more than she had today.

"There are many," said Asti. "Remember, we are not bound by a fence and neatly cut grass. We stretch out for many miles up and down the river. Some cats even live at the bottom of Storm Water Falls, where it's dark and damp and very dangerous. They never come up here, but many cats have seen them from the tops of the trees above the falls, wandering in and out of the tunnels, feeding off rats and dead birds. You can only see this when the river is very low and the falls are a trickle. Rumour has it that Tafari is the only cat from up here to have actually been down there and returned. But then, many are the legends surrounding the prince."

"Why doesn't he ever come to the assemblies at the complex?" asked Tikana. "Most of the cats think he is just a myth. I have only ever seen him once before today. He is so big and handsome..." Her voice trailed off as if she were going into a trance.

"Tikana," purred Asti, bringing her back into the moment, "Tafari has no owner now. He was raised as a tame cat, but his royal blood line, domestic mother, and wild cat father made him independent—too independent. When his owners were moving, they searched for him for days, desperate that he should return home before they packed up to leave. He never did, and they had to leave without him. When Tafari returned home, someone new had moved into the apartment. Some said he was hiding on purpose, longing to be wild; others said he was heartbroken. From that day on, the River Glades Cats saw very little of him."

PC listened, and before he knew it, blurted out, "But where does he sleep?"

Asti smiled. "He has a den on the banks of the river, north of the estate. All the tomcats that he has put in charge meet him there sometimes, to discuss matters and the running of the estate and the river."

Asti continued chatting and telling tales of life at the river until PC fell asleep from sheer exhaustion.

Seeing that PC was asleep, Tikana hesitantly whispered one last question to Asti. "Does Tafari...I mean, is Tafari...well, does he love anyone special?"

Asti laughed, and then purred, "No, Tafari has no bride as yet. There are only a few pure royal cats left in the River Lands. He must take a royal bride, royal in blood and character. Tafari is not like the other princes along the River Lands; he loves the tame cats as well as the wild cats, as if they were all his precious ones. Only far away in the wild are there true wild cat princes. Most of the domestic princes will not even speak to a cat like me—a wild cat, that is. They look down on us. In their territories cats like Jake and Jethro rule the wild cats with violence and fear. Not so here under Tafari's rule. He has taught many of the wild cats to act more nobly than some of those princes. He always believes in us and loves us, even when we choose not to believe in what he says about us. He always says, 'Cats were born to be free and noble.'" Asti paused. She had a faraway look in her eyes.

"There was a cat once, a beautiful blue Siamese, on the estate. Her blood was pure royalty, and Tafari was very much in love with her. But she would never think of talking to any of the wild cats Tafari loved so much. She was afraid of us. You see, we can never love those we are afraid of. Her fear kept her a prisoner inside the estate. When her owners packed up ready to move to a large house further up the river, Tafari begged her to stay with him down at the river. She wouldn't, and it broke his heart."

Asti became silent for a long time after that, until Tikana asked, "Asti, do you think he will make it?"

Asti looked out over the river. "He always does."

CHAPTER EIGHTEEN

As soon as Buzz leapt from the spinning branches, they whipped upward and then crashed down hard, back towards the river, spinning even faster. Tafari could feel the branches start to splinter and break beneath him. He realized he must manoeuvre back up and onto the trunk. But if he could keep his weight on the spinning branches, they would snap before Jethro got to him, taking Jethro back down into the whirlpool below. If he timed it perfectly, Tafari could leap to safety. His mind was spinning faster than the branches he was clinging to—a split second too late or too early would be his end.

Snap! One of the branches gave way. Jethro heard it and increased his efforts to climb faster to safety. Tafari turned his body around, dropped all of his weight, and leapt into the adjacent branches, grasping whatever he could hold onto. It was the end of the spinning branches. The sudden side swish put too much strain on the taut, twisted wood, and the remaining two branches snapped, sending Jethro hurtling backwards into the rising pool. He was rapidly carried down into the third pool and disappeared under the water.

Tafari made his way quickly along the tops of the trees until he was over the falls. He was just in time to see Jethro climb onto the ledge at the bottom of Storm Water Falls and slink away into the dark tunnel.

CHAPTER NINETEEN

 cold splash of water woke Buzz, and he felt his body being pulled higher up the rocks.

"Tafari?" Buzz whispered, unable to speak louder. The river was bathed in green and yellow as the sun set through the storm clouds, lighting them up as it went.

"You did well," said Tafari, pressing his paw against Buzz. "Jethro is gone."

"Did he...?" Buzz paused suddenly, unable to get the word out.

"No Buzz, he is not dead, but dead to us. He will not try to come back up Storm Water Falls, not while I am prince, and now with Tikana—" He stopped suddenly.

Buzz stood, albeit shakily. "What was that you were saying about the princess?" He used the word "princess" like he always had, in a teasing, sarcastic tone. But the look on Tafari's face silenced him, and made him feel full of remorse at how he had teased her. Tafari's stare was not cruel, but cut so deep into Buzz's heart that he felt sorry for her and mad with her at the same time. Buzz swallowed hard and looked down.

"Being true to who you really are is difficult, Buzz. Some cats are born royal but never act that way. Tikana is true to who she really is, even though she doesn't know her ancestry and is unsure of herself." Then he looked up at the stars and back down at Buzz. "Tikana comes from one of the purest royal bloodlines there is. She is a real princess."

He motioned with his head towards the falls.

"Jethro too comes from a royal bloodline. But he allowed bitterness and hatred to take over his appearance. You saw how he changed when he held the statue."

Buzz recalled how large and overpowering he had seemed back at the den.

"There is no real power in the statue—only the power of remembrance. When those with royal blood are in possession of one, they remember who they really are. Unfortunately the statue has no power to change their hearts if they are dark already. Owning a statue will simply make a wicked cat think they have the right to rule with cruelty.

Buzz's curiosity was nearly undoing him, and a thousand questions started to fill his mind. There was something far deeper and more mysterious about being royal, but before he could ask anything, Tafari motioned to him to follow. "We may need the backup of tonight's sentries. Jake is unpredictable. The others could be in danger."

Buzz knew the guards and where they patrolled like the back of his hand. There had been many times he had managed to slip past them. "We need to hurry to Stonewall Lookout. Tonight's sentries will be there by now."

The two walked quickly and carefully, Buzz starting to feel the pain of his cuts and bruises.

CHAPTER TWENTY

PC had not been asleep for long when he awoke. He loved the yellow-green light after a storm and started to dart this way and that, catching imaginary prey hiding in the overhanging willow branches.

Tikana and Asti sat on the flat rock, staring up at the painted sky. The wind was dying down, and the clouds parted slightly. The river was a distant roar, now completely flooded from the storm.

"Today felt like a year," said Tikana. Her life back in the glades seemed so far removed from what she had been through. The sky seemed wider and the horizon further away than that morning. The willow trees at the river, which had always seemed so tall to her, were now smaller.

"You have grown worlds," said Asti.

Tikana wondered why Asti always sounded so mysterious and decided it was because she used words like they were toys. They had no control over her. She used them in such a magical way, like puppets dancing in a play.

"How do you grow worlds?" asked Tikana.

"Growing worlds," said Asti, "is when you suddenly see differently, as though someone switched on a light or opened the curtain. I am not sure why, but it has nothing to do with your eyesight, you know." Tikana blinked a few times, sure she was seeing with her eyes. Asti laughed at her then turned suddenly to PC. "Someone's coming; quickly PC, over here!"

The three cats crouched down low in the bushes next to the flat rock. No one appeared.

"Are you sure someone's coming?" Tikana whispered.

"Certain. Look up in that willow."

Tikana could see nothing but wind moving the tree.

The grey sky was growing darker and all the shadows around the trees started to look like cats.

"Night is coming," whispered Asti. "I was so certain...we must try to get back to the fence. The river is no place for tame cats in the moonlight." She turned to Tikana, but Tikana wasn't listening; her body had been frozen by the scent in her nose.

"Tikana, are you all right?" asked PC.

At that moment Asti picked up the scent, but it was too late. Down from the willow trees above them descended Jake and the blue-eyed stray cat, circling them with eyes aflame.

76

CHAPTER TWENTY ONE

Y our heroes deserted you, ladies?" hissed Jake

PC went red with rage. He was no she-cat! Oh how he wished he could magically grow and fight them back.

Jake spat in Asti's face. "Who are the cowards now?" he hissed. Asti winced and wiped her cheek. Silence was now her only weapon. They would never be able to defend themselves against two of the largest and meanest cats at the river.

"Where's your prince now, Princess?" they jeered at Tikana.

Tikana remained frozen almost like a statue, but she felt a strength inside of her starting to well up, making its way into her mouth.

"Only cowards attack those who are weaker than themselves," said Tikana, her voice quite steady.

Jake came back at her, his face pressed up against her and his paws around her neck. "What did you call me?" he hissed.

Still Tikana was unmoved. "A coward," she said again, quite clearly. "A coward is a cat who has no real belief in himself, only in the power of metal and stone."

Asti, although she was indeed wishing that she had said that to Jake, saw the gap and, with Jake's paws around Tikana, jumped up onto Flat Rock. She hoped that his sidekick would follow her, giving PC a chance to run away and get help.

Like lightning, Jake was on top of her, pinning her down.

"Run!" she screamed to PC. "Run towards the lights!"

As Jake glanced up, Tikana sank her claw into his back paw. The pain made him release his grip on her. At that moment PC, still infuriated with Jake for calling him a girl, flung himself upon Jake's head, knocking him off balance, and bit down into his ear.

Dazed for a second, Jake pulled PC off and flung him towards Flat Rock. He landed with a thud and lay still.

"PC!" screamed Asti, still pinned down by the grey cat. She wrestled as hard as she could to get free but could only watch in horror as Jake strode towards his limp little body. Tikana, struggling to breathe after Jake's grip around her neck, tried to hold him back, but he flung her off. With his claws readied for a death blow, he moved towards PC. Asti struggled with all her might, claws and fangs grasping the air.

Jake lifted his paw above PC just as he was coming around. He opened his eyes, cowered, and, instead of feeling a deathblow, felt the smothering of fur and weight of a cat on top of him.

It was Buzz. He and Tafari had come from the giant oaks near Stonewall Lookout and snuck up from behind Flat Rock. In an instant Buzz knew what Jake would do. It was his signature strike, the death blow. Buzz had even witnessed it one terrible night when he had stumbled into a trader's fight. There had been only one victor.

Without thinking, Buzz had whizzed past Asti and her captor, meeting Jake's paw in mid-air. He landed with a thud on top of PC.

The next few seconds were a flurry of rolling fights and wild cat cries. Buzz and Tafari had only been able to find one sentry, who immediately went for Jake. Tafari released Asti and had the grey cat begging for mercy as they tied him to a nearby willow tree.

The sentry, although larger than Jake and fearless, was no match for Jake's fighting skills, and one powerful scratch to his head had him stumble and slip down the bank between two trees on the opposite side of the grassy circle. It was Jake's golden opportunity.

Leaping for Tikana, who was heading over to Buzz and PC, he grabbed her again by the throat. With one paw over her mouth he hissed, "Going somewhere, Princess? "

Tikana was quite overcome with fear and gave a muffled cry, biting down into Jake's paw. Jake only tightened his grip.

Tafari turned around. "Let her go, Jake," he commanded.

"Let her go?" Jake spat. "When I can have my own real life statue?" His eyes were wild and evil.

"I said let her go." Tafari spoke almost calmly now, with an authority that came from very deep inside. "There is no honour in living a life of deception. True royalty comes from inside, not from owning a statue. Some cats are born with it; others become nobler from their actions than royalty itself. Let her go, and I will let you live, albeit in the banished lands on the other side of the river."

But Jake's heart could not be won over. He had given it away already, to bitterness and hatred. They had authority now, and his actions had to obey them. He turned to Tikana and stared into her face. Her beauty and stature were quite beyond anything he had ever seen. It was almost as if he had gone into a trance, his one paw around her delicate neck. For a moment her beauty almost melted his heart. But then the thought of her not being his to possess was too much for him and an ancient rage welled up inside him. His anger overcame everything, and it grew bigger than him. He began to tighten his grip around her neck and she started to choke.

Tafari had given him a chance but was not going to risk losing Tikana. He had witnessed many a fight of Jake's. A great cry broke the night as Tafari flew at Jake, crushing him into Flat Rock, the force of the blow knocking Tikana out of his grip. Jake's body crumpled to the ground and lay still.

CHAPTER TWENTY TWO

The silence that fell was dark and momentary. The sky parted for stars, and far in the distance, the lights of the homes in the River Glades Estate flickered.

Asti was the first to fly into action. Next to the crumpled body of Jake was Buzz and underneath him a slowly suffocating PC. Quickly, Asti and the sentry, who had managed to climb back up the hill, pulled Buzz off PC.

Buzz, although still unconscious, moaned and swore at them, even though he later denied this. PC, who had fainted from a lack of oxygen, quickly came around and looked up at the stars. He clung onto Asti.

"Hush, fearful one," she said in her most soothing and hypnotic voice. "Peace has been restored. Tafari has won back the River Lands. Breathe in courage, and breathe out your fear."

Tafari knelt beside Tikana, who was coughing and gasping for air. Gently he wiped a tear off her cheek and then lifted her up. He pressed his head up against her until her coughing stopped and she could breathe again. Then he looked straight into her eyes.

"I am so sorry that you had to witness death tonight. You have been so brave, Tikana, Princess of the Southern Cross, daughter of Alnitak the Fearless and Miltaka the Graceful." And with that he bowed low.

Deep inside Tikana felt a rising; was it a memory or an emotion or something even deeper in her being? She was not sure. But it was full of hope and power and peace.

Almost without thinking, the other cats bowed their heads, and a great stillness came over them.

It was completely dark now, and the bush at the river was full of night sounds. Crickets and frogs croaked as though nothing unusual had happened, and there was even the sound of wild cats further down the river. In the distance a dog barked and a plover bird called to its mate.

The small party of cats circled around Jake's body.

Tafari saluted the sentry, who stood to attention, awaiting his orders.

"Go and find the border crossing sentries. They will need to escort the prisoner across to the banished lands and bury Jake. I will escort the others back to the fence." The sentry nodded and saluted the prince.

The small group turned away. No one was up to climbing trees, so they stayed on the ground. Tafari led the way in silence.

After what seemed like an age, lights began to appear through the trees, and a voice called out suddenly, "Halt. Who goes there?"

It was Titanic, the sentry on the night watch.

"Nothing to fear," replied Tafari. "Permission to come through the fence?"

"Your Majesty," gasped Titanic. "There are rumours across the glades that you are dead."

"I am quite well," replied Tafari, unwilling to give details of the day. "Permission to pass?"

"Yes, of course, Your Majesty," said Titanic, saluting the prince as he passed by, his jaw dropping when he noticed the rest of the party, but he said nothing. After they had all crept through the fence, Tafari called Titanic close.

"No rumours, please. Let's just keep this to ourselves for now," he whispered.

"Yes," Titanic replied, almost bursting with curiosity. Tafari, trusting his faithful guard, added, "There has been a death, a banishment, and an escape down Storm Water Falls. Assemble the toms tomorrow at the bluff for a meeting."

"The bluff, Your Majesty?" questioned Titanic, but Tafari gave no reason for the change of venue.

The toms always met at Willow Tree Point, as the bluff was right at the fence and not very private. It was a point at which the river and the fence came within metres of each other, where many illegal fish trades and a lot of card games happened.

"Leave it to me," replied Titanic.

CHAPTER TWENTY THREE

They continued up the grassy bank towards the buildings, little paved courtyards, and garden fences. There were lights along the pathway now, and walking became easier.

Buzz lifted his paw at the first courtyard, unable to speak. Tafari nodded good night, his eyes saying so much more. The complex was alive with visitors and music, people strolling along the paths and flashing lights from television sets. Asti darted between the shadows of the bushes next to the path until eventually she stopped altogether.

"Tafari," she whispered, "if Tikana can take PC the rest of the way, I would like to go home now." She nuzzled PC and licked him on the head.

PC looked at her, puzzled, until Tikana pressed her paw on his and said, "I would be very pleased to complete my task. We have had enough adventure for one day!"

She turned to Asti, her new friend. But Tikana felt a pang of grief as she realized that she would almost never see a wild cat friend.

Asti brushed her whiskers against Tikana's. "Today we have been friends, but soon I shall be your servant. If ever you need help, I will be close by. This I vow." She bowed before Tikana and pressed paw upon paw before stepping back into the darkness.

"I will escort you home, Asti," called Tafari, and with that he bowed his head and looked Tikana straight in the eyes, as though he wanted to say something but couldn't. Then he disappeared into the dark night.

An unfamiliar feeling came over Tikana, and she found it difficult to focus for a few moments. She felt a deep excitement and hurt all at the same time, and a million questions came to mind. Her head started to spin. Eventually PC brought her back to reality by pulling on her front leg. She turned to him and whispered, "Come. Let's go home, and no shortcuts this time!"

PC was almost asleep by the time they got to his apartment. He was so tired that Tikana had to lift him up through the cat flap. She pushed it open, pushed him through, and heard him roll onto the floor below. Silence. He had obviously fallen into a deep sleep right where he landed. She stood outside his door for ages and then stumbled down the stairs and back into the blurry courtyard.

"Well, well, well, if it isn't the tour guide," a voice came booming in her ear. It was Magnum, all puffed up and official. "Princess," he continued sarcastically, "perhaps you haven't heard, but there has been a lot of trouble at the river today, and the prince has ordered a curfew tonight, which you are breaking! This is a very serious matter, and I have been given orders to arrest anyone who breaks it!"

"I know," she said quickly. "I am on my way home now." And she heaved herself off in the direction of home, her heart pounding. Magnum watched as she limped through her doorway.

CHAPTER TWENTY FOUR

The morning light streaked onto the bed where Tikana was sleeping. She stretched and purred, blinking. Restless, she had woken several times with nightmares, thinking she could hear wild cats outside her window. The sun was already high, and she realized that she had slept late into the morning. She rolled over and jerked as her body ached.

Just a day had changed her life forever. It had started so normally and ended with her in a new world.

She staggered over to the basin and looked in the mirror. She was bruised and swollen around her neck. A sip of water was sheer agony to swallow. Dizzy, she lay down again until she felt strong enough to eat something. Her supper was stale in her bowl. Ravenous, she gulped it down, stiffening up from the pain of each mouthful.

Was she really a princess? Or was that part a dream? Her thoughts turned to Tafari, and she felt a rush inside that she didn't understand and a deep longing to see him.

Tikana jumped up onto the windowsill and looked out across the river. Exhausted, she was soon back on her chair, lying down. So much had happened—too much to take in. Her eyes closed, and sleep once again covered her.

CHAPTER TWENTY FIVE

Hours later, when it was dark again, Tikana awoke to the sound of laughing down in the courtyard. She was still very stiff but managed to slip out through the cat flap and onto the balcony where she could get a good look at what was going on. It was Buzz and a group of young toms. Buzz was entertaining them with stories and jokes. Tikana strained her eyes. He looked different, but she couldn't see why until he moved into the light. He had been shaved in patches all over his body and stitched up in many places. The younger toms were all admiring his battle scars, and Tikana was sure Buzz would be making up stories to go along with them.

She crept up closer, hoping to listen unnoticed.

"And at that moment," said Buzz, "I leapt to safety and..."

Tikana sneezed, revealing her cover. Pairs of eyes moved in her direction.

"Wanting to join the conversation, Princess?" sneered one of the toms.

"Tried to swallow your crown?" laughed another.

Buzz just stared at her, speechless. Unable to protect her and his reputation at the same time, he looked away and tried to ignore her. The toms circled Tikana, lifting the hair on her back. They laughed and hissed as she crouched low. She closed her eyes as their breath moved her whiskers.

"Boys!" called Buzz, pretending to laugh, "give her a break. Besides, I haven't finished my story yet."

"You're not going soft, are you, Buzz?" mewed one of the toms.

Buzz rose to an unfamiliar size and struck out with a claw. The tom shrank low, hissing and defensive. Further away from Buzz, a tom flicked his tail in Tikana's face, his eyes burning through her fur.

"I'm not sure your story can bring quite as much pleasure as a game with Her Majesty," he hissed.

"Probably not," mewed Buzz, realising he was too sore for another fight, "but an injured princess is not fair game."

"And when was the last time you played fair?" the tom hissed back.

"Fair comment," whispered Tikana.

Buzz squinted at her and then turned to walk away. Seizing the opportunity, the toms circled in once more, tails swirling and flicking. One of them flicked her bruised tail like it was a dead snake.

"No, please!" Tikana wailed in pain.

Buzz stopped and held his breath. Swishing some leaves off the path with his tail, he limped back.

"Knew you couldn't resist a game with Her Majesty, Buzz," one of the toms hissed on Buzz's return.

"Come, Tikana," choked Buzz. "I'll walk you home."

The toms' heads tilted at Buzz questioningly.

"Not until she tells us why she swallowed her crown," jeered one of them.

"Come on, Your Majesty!" mocked another.

"Yes?" Came a deep voice from behind them. It was Tafari. He stepped out of the shadows, his fur glistening with dew.

The young toms were swallowing and side stepping.

"Quickly, be off with you!" ordered Tafari.

They scattered in all directions, leaving the three cats alone in the courtyard.

"Follow me," whispered Tafari. "Let's go where we will not be spied on."

Tikana felt her heart pounding in her chest and could not speak, but she was quick to follow and soon forgot about her aching body.

The three cats slipped out of the courtyard and along the path towards one of the swimming pools. Tafari jumped up into a nearby tree and walked along the branches, leaping onto the gazebo roof. The stars were smudgy and the night very still.

Buzz and Tikana followed him until he came to rest, right at the top of the gazebo. Tikana kept her eyes downcast, not wanting to meet the prince's gaze.

Tafari launched straight into business. "I must speak to both of you about very important matters. The air down at the river is thick with rumour and tension. There is a jostling for position now that Jake and Jethro are no longer around. I will need to focus my attention on the River Lands for a few weeks and have left Magnum in charge of the estate."

Tikana felt all hope drop out of her heart, but she tried not to show it. She knew at that moment that she was falling in love with him. Her mind raced, quick conversations whizzing around her head. Part of her knew that most of the females in the complex were "in love" with Tafari; some of them had never even seen him and were "in love" with him. Others swooned whenever he came to the meetings, and there was fierce arguing as to who he would one day choose as a bride. How silly she was to think he would even notice her! After all, he may have saved her life and called her a princess, but they had not spoken as one would to a friend. She didn't know anything about him really, except what Asti had told her and what she had observed.

"Tikana?" Tafari's voice was soft as he turned towards her. She was startled and realized that she had not been able to hide her disappointment. Her eyes were welling up with tears, and her pain was returning.

"Tikana? What is it?" asked Buzz suspiciously.

"Nothing," said Tikana, trying to brush Buzz aside, but her body was aching terribly, and she started shaking.

Tikana suddenly felt alone. She knew she was being ridiculous, but it was all so overwhelming. Old feelings of abandonment started to suck at her breath. Ridicule and rumour watched from the shadows, ready to pounce.

Almost as if he could read her mind, Tafari looked deep into her eyes. "You have suffered so much provocation and rejection," he said. "You are struggling to see who you really are. You are a princess, Tikana. Your blood is royal and your heart noble. Don't be afraid." His words warmed her and planted hope.

"How long will you be gone?" Tikana asked hesitantly.

"I cannot tell," mewed Tafari. Then he turned towards Buzz and placed his paw on Buzz's paw. "I am appointing you to be Tikana's bodyguard."

Buzz pulled back his paw and looked at Tikana. They gasped together at Tafari...

"What?"

Tikana's head started to spin, and her breathing became shallow.

"But Your Majesty," said Buzz quickly, "I am nothing but a scoundrel and a river trader. I can't protect her."

"He can't protect me," added Tikana quickly. "He—"

Tafari interrupted them. "Buzz saved my life, Tikana, and I am entrusting you to him. He is one of the bravest cats I know."

Tikana sat down, dizzy and speechless.

Tafari continued, "You both need to lie low for a while and let your wounds heal. Order must be returned to the river for the sake of all the cats—especially the cats within the estate. There will be a meeting at the next full moon. I hope to see you then."

He raised his paw to touch Tikana's swollen neck. She flinched and moved away.

"I am so sorry," he whispered. "When you are better and things have settled, I'd like to show you a different view of the river. It's not the place you may think it is..." His voice trailed off. He looked deep into her heart as if he was going to smile and say more, but a hardness came over him, and he turned and started walking away.

"Look after her well, Buzz," he said, and he jumped from the roof onto a nearby tree and disappeared into the blackness.

Buzz and Tikana kept an uncomfortable and silent space between them as they made their way home. Reaching Tikana's door, they stopped and sat down, both staring ahead. It was Buzz who turned at last towards Tikana.

"Goodnight, Princess." He grinned and bowed. "Sweet dreams, and no wandering around without me."

Tikana was about to reply when Buzz flew across the courtyard, and she was left alone again. She felt so frustrated. The meeting had been so short and not what she was expecting at all! Tafari had seemed so distant, even though he had told her he wanted to show her the river. But perhaps all new princesses got 'shown' around the river. Tikana lay awake for hours thinking about the evening's events and reliving them in her mind. Eventually she fell asleep, quite dissatisfied.

ikana stayed indoors for days. She even stayed away from the windows until one afternoon when she could hear a commotion downstairs. Leaping onto the windowsill, she peered through the glass. It was PC. He had caught his first bird but was at the same time being chased by a Jack Russell who had him perched precariously up on a small fence. The weight of the bird in his mouth was soon to topple him down into the jaws of the Jack Russell. Tikana rushed back inside and out of her doorway. She knew she needed to distract the dog so PC could escape. Running outside and down the steps, she crashed straight into Buzz, who was watching with great amusement.

"Buzz," scolded Tikana, "he needs our help! "

"All right," said Buzz, "but we run together. I have my orders. On my count. One, two, three!" The two cats ran past the Jack Russell, who immediately left PC and gave chase.

"Let's lead him to the geese!" called Buzz. "Just follow me!"

The cats sped down the paths, over driveways and gardens, until they came to an open patch of grass near the fence where the geese would waddle.

"At my signal," instructed Buzz, "we split and jump for the trees at the fence."

Their plan worked, and the Jack Russell turned on the geese, barking furiously.

Tikana charged up a giant oak tree, just high enough to get a view of the river. It was gloriously sunny, and it felt so good to be out in the fresh air. Very soon Buzz was at her side. They looked at each other and laughed.

"I thought you were never going to appear," said Buzz.

"Have you been waiting all these days for me?" asked Tikana, a little embarrassed.

"Well," said Buzz, "I was told to look after you by the prince himself!"

"Yes, you were," replied Tikana. "Are you better?"

"I'm feeling fantastic." said Buzz. "And you? You look beautiful."

The word just came out unexpectedly, and Tikana blushed.

"Thanks, Buzz. I never thought I would hear you say that!"

"Neither did I," said Buzz quickly.

A silence fell between them, awkward and suffocating. Buzz sharpened his claws on the tree branch and looked out over the river.

"Sometimes," said Buzz, breaking the silence, "we don't think about why we are saying things or acting in a certain way. Then it becomes part of us and is the only response we can find." He looked down before continuing. "I have always thought that you were lovely, Tikana—lovely and completely out of my reach. Pride can be a very safe friend when we don't feel good enough. But pride does have sharp teeth, and I have—"

Tikana interrupted, touching Buzz on his paw. "I forgive you, Buzz; it's in the past." Her words were abrupt but brought a satisfying close to a conversation Buzz never thought he would have to have.

"I can see that PC is happy!" said Tikana, changing the subject. "I've actually missed him."

"He is quite the kitten," said Buzz. "Yesterday I had to teach him a quick lesson on Hadedas and geese! Ever since his adventure, he thinks he is much bigger than he really is and can't stop boasting about the fact that he is most probably the only kitten ever to have been to the river and survived."

"With thanks to you," said Tikana. "It wasn't only the prince's life you saved!" Buzz looked at her, and their eyes met properly for the first time in years.

"PC is quite the storyteller," Buzz added, looking casually out at the view again.

"I'm sure that is earning him quite a reputation for telling lies!" mewed Tikana. "It sounds like he needs looking after."

"Well, there are plenty of she-cats running after him and keeping an eye on him," laughed Buzz.

The tree was high up over the fence, and the two cats noticed some movement on the other side. It was Magnum talking to a mixed group of toms, some from the complex, some wild.

Tikana moved closer to try to hear what was being said. Buzz followed; they crouched low and held still.

"Not a meeting for a princess." A voice startled Tikana from far above her, and she looked up. She could see nothing but branches. Odd, she thought. Buzz didn't seem to have heard anything, and his curiosity had got the better of him. He was now much lower than Tikana in the tree.

A leaf floated past Tikana's ear, and then she knew the voice was Asti!

"I know you're here," she whispered back.

"Higher and higher!" came the reply. Still Tikana couldn't see a thing, but up she climbed. The branches were thick and the leaves dense in the old oak. Cautiously Tikana made her way towards the direction of the voice. Then at last she spotted a dark blue-black tail, hanging almost invisible in the branch shadows.

"Found you!" gasped Tikana as she leapt up next to Asti.

Asti grinned but remained quite still. "Keeping one's body completely still," said Asti "is half the disguise." Then she turned towards Tikana and smiled. "Regal friend, are you well?" and she placed her paw on Tikana's.

Tikana grinned back. Asti had called her 'friend'. "I have healed, thank you. Not sure I am going to enjoy being followed by Buzz everywhere." And she looked down through the branches to see if he was on his way after her.

"From whom have you been hiding?" asked Asti. "Yourself, perhaps?"

Tikana wished she was invisible but then felt that Asti would most probably still be able to see her even if she were transparent.

"Asti," she said, hesitating, "I have lived with rejection my whole life. I have never had friends or family, and no tomcats have ever even glanced at me...well, unless they were teasing me. I suspect I am not even sure how to be a true friend. Ever since that night at the river, I feel so unsure of everything. And then there's Tafari. I have such deep feelings inside about him and who he says I am, but I am afraid of them and of more rejection. So you are right, I guess. I have been hiding—in uncertainty and fear."

"A waterfall of words," smiled Asti. Then she paused and asked, "Do you remember your mother, Tikana?"

"Yes, but only in dreams and in flashes of memory, like pictures that are fading. There are some things she told me before she left, but even those are so faint, I can hardly hear them anymore. That golden statue that fell into the river was so like her. When I look at my reflection I can see nothing of her, only her colouring."

"That is because you reflect more of your father."

Tikana looked at Asti in amazement. "You knew my father?"

"Yes. Your father and his love for the beautiful in this world." Her eyes glazed for a moment as she spoke. "We were both in love with beautiful things and words." Then she became very present and turned towards Tikana. "Our families were against our friendship, wild cat and domestic cat. When your mother came to the estate, there was no question that she should be his bride."

"But Tafari has a domestic mother and a wild cat father," mewed Tikana.

"The first ever union of wild cat prince and domestic princess. But his father was pure royal wild cat. Not like the wild cats around here. Asti paused before carrying on. "Alnitak soon became prince, and our friendship had to change."

"What was he like?" asked Tikana, trying to hide her surprise.

"Alnitak was tall, lean and muscular; the fastest runner in the land and a pure golden Abyssinian. He loved the river and his wild cat friends. Although Tafari was able to bring peace, your father made it possible. He broke the lies that wild cats had spread about domestic cats and domestic cats had spread about wild cats. He placed sentinels at the gate to stop wild cat raids and introduced fair trading. All the young wild cat females were in love with him. When he chose your mother as a bride, everyone grieved so. But they were happy together and loved life at the river. And soon enough, all the cats loved your mother as well as Alnitak."

"I wish I could have known him on this side of the stars," sighed Tikana.

Asti got a distant look on her face again and looked up through the branches. Then she carried on speaking as though there were words that had to come out—words that had been lodged in her heart for years.

"One summer it rained and rained for weeks, causing the river to become brown and polluted. Every day the river rose higher, carrying with it toxins and debris. Many of the families along the riverbank became sick and had to move away, and many dens were flooded. The rain was unrelenting, and one evening a litter of newborn kittens got washed into the river. Your father saved them, each and every one, including the mother. But he swallowed too much water, and it made him sick. It was only a few days later that he died.

"Why would he do that?" asked Tikana, feeling indignant. "Rescue wild kittens and risk his life!" Asti looked hurt, but only for a brief moment, and Tikana realized what she had said. Horrified by her attitude and perhaps the attitude most domestic cats had towards wild cats, Tikana tried desperately to apologize. "Oh Asti, I am so sorry. I didn't mean that he shouldn't have—I-I…"

Tikana became silent. Nothing could take back her words. She knew she would have done the same and was so surprised by her own response. Tears welled up in her eyes, and she looked away.

"You have lost much, Tikana," said Asti. "Sometimes when we are too young to grieve, anger sneaks up on us when we are grown up. Anger can have a mouth that surprises our tongues."

"I think you should be the princess and not me," sniffed Tikana. "How would I ever rule wisely and graciously? My mother said that some cats are more noble than royalty itself, and you Asti, are one of those cats."

Asti smiled. "Perhaps royal by heart, but not royal by blood. No Tikana. You have your father's heart as well as his good looks. You are of very pure royal blood. Wisdom will come to you, and your heart will receive it because it is open. The cats in the complex have twisted your true identity and used it to try to break you. But their words can never take from you who you really are. Now that you know your true identity, it will not be long before you believe it, and fear will leave you."

Asti paused. "There is one more thing." She looked down as if it was Tikana who needed to forgive her. "The mother of the kittens your father rescued was me."

Tikana was speechless, and all she could do was press her face against Asti's and weep.

CHAPTER TWENTY SEVEN

uzz crept very quietly to a branch where he could hear what the toms were talking about and still remain hidden.

"If Tafari is to choose a princess, there must be proof. There has always been proof, a golden statue of the princess or her parents in her possession." Magnum was clearly in charge of the gathering and continued, "Just because a she-cat is golden in colour doesn't make her royal!"

"Hear, hear!" agreed some of the older toms.

"There has never been a royal marriage without proof!" added one of the senior sentinels. "I propose we give Tafari's princess an ultimatum. Find your statues, from both parents, or face banishment for pretending to be royal and making advances towards the prince!"

Buzz's head was spinning; they must be talking about Tikana. Then he remembered he was not supposed to leave her side—prince's orders. Buzz hissed under his breath and looked around for her. He really wanted to continue eavesdropping but knew he would have to go and find Tikana soon. He decided to listen for just a few more minutes.

"I am deeply grieved," said Titanic, Tafari's most faithful friend and servant. "The way you are all talking is disrespectful. Tafari has brought peace to our lands, and now, just because of tradition, you would deny him a bride because she has no proof of royalty. Tafari himself has only one statue, from his father, the greatest wild cat prince the Western River Lands has ever had. And we all know it was his mother's choice to give her statue to his brother Jethro."

"We are not asking for two statues. One has always been sufficient," interrupted an older tom. "To ask for two statues is ridiculous."

"His mother was an Abyssinian, domestic, golden, just like the princess," broke in another tom.

"Her decision to make her sons equal was a poor one. When greed took over Jethro's heart, he sold his birth right to the evil Lord Anak for the River Crossing Territories. Without a statue he could no longer prove his royalty, and he has been trying to get one ever since."

Buzz thrust his paw over his face in shock. Was Jethro really Tafari's brother? No wonder he was so desperate for the golden statue, having sold his birthright for a piece of land.

"Brothers," continued the senior sentry, "if Tafari takes a bride without a statue, the royal line is weakened yet again."

"But Tafari is the eldest son of two pure royal lines," insisted Titanic. "It's not his fault his mother made a poor decision. She has regretted it ever since. Jethro sold not only his title for a piece of earth but his soul to the wild cats at the River Crossing—all for wealth. Now he's forever to roam the dark beneath Storm Water Falls."

"Don't be so sure of that," spat Magnum. "Tafari himself has been down there and come back. If Jethro returns and Tafari has taken a bride without proof of royalty, there will be a war. We must insist." Then he lowered his voice so that Buzz had to strain with all his might to hear.

"I will not be humiliated again by that 'princess'. She must know that the toms rule above her."

"No, Magnum," interrupted Titanic. "What you are speaking is treason, and I will have none of it."

Magnum grabbed Titanic by the throat to a wild hissing and growling of toms. "One word of this to Tafari, and I'll kill you myself."

"Enough!" roared the most senior sentinel present. "Magnum, release him! You are losing your mind. We are all on the side of the prince. Now control yourself! Perhaps Tafari should have thought twice before leaving you in charge."

Magnum retreated but kept his gaze fast on Titanic.

"What has been discussed here is a matter of the council of toms and will not be repeated to the prince. That is the way it has always been. We are his council, not his servants."

"That is where you are wrong Magnum. I serve the prince as a friend and brother. I consider it a privilege, and whoever he chooses to take as a bride I shall serve also. Besides, the council has never met without Tafari." With that, Titanic turned and walked away.

"This is not an official meeting anyway," Magnum called after him, looking at the toms for support. Their silence isolated him, and one by one they dispersed into the undergrowth.

Buzz was clawed to the branch, and it took him a few minutes to really take in what had been discussed. He would mention not a word of it to Tikana.

But already he was making plans of his own. He would wait a few days until it was almost full moon.

"Oh, there you are, Buzz! Still in the same place I left you," meowed Tikana, landing next to him. Buzz, still motionless, got the fright of his life but tried not to show it.

"Why are you looking so disturbed? Find out anything interesting?"

"No," answered Buzz, irritated.

Tikana was puzzled. "Buzz? You look odd."

"And you have been crying," he said, trying to change the subject.

Tikana looked away, not wanting to discuss the past hour with Buzz.

Buzz breathed a sigh of relief and started to walk in the direction of home.

CHAPTER TWENTY EIGHT

The sun was turning a dark orange when Tikana stretched and pulled herself from slumber. Yawning, she jumped onto the windowsill.

"Buzz!" she shrieked as he leapt up onto the ledge outside at exactly the same time as her. He had his trading bag slung over his shoulder. Tikana squinted in the sun, jumped down, and went out through the cat flap in the door.

"Where have you been?" Buzz whined. "I really need to—"

"Go trading?" interrupted Tikana.

"Well, yes. But there is no need for you to even be seen." Buzz looked down and took a deep breath. "I really am sorry about last time. I—"

"It's in the past," Tikana clipped. "I'll come."

Buzz flew down the stairs with Tikana running a few paces behind. Many cats were heading down towards the river, and Buzz led Tikana a long way around to avoid being seen.

Trade Point Wall was purring with cats. Tikana arched her back and closed her eyes.

"You don't need to come any further, Tikana. Wait here in these trees," mewed Buzz, a short way off. Tikana leapt sideways and was gone. Buzz hesitated for a moment, looked back, and then set his course for the high trees to the right of Trade Point Wall. Trading had already begun. A sentry moved gracefully along the top of the wall, announcing the wild cat's bounty.

"Twelve river fish is today's catch."

The cats jostled for position, holding up all kinds of trinkets.

Buzz bounced on an overhanging branch, releasing a spray of leaves onto the crowd. It was his sign to the wild cats to look up and hopefully choose to trade privately with him further down the boundary fence. He caught the eye of a wild she-cat who was clutching two river fish.

"Perfect." Buzz motioned to her, and she slipped from the wild trading crowd.

Down through the trees Buzz darted and crept along the wall, making sure no one spotted him. At the point where the wall ended and just a palisade fence continued, Buzz jumped into the River Lands beyond the border of the estate. He camouflaged himself in the bushes and waited.

"Buzz," hissed a voice, "where are you?"

Buzz tentatively peered out of the bushes, his nose telling him a trade was at hand. The exchange was quick. Two fish for a small silver chain. No words and only a flash of eye contact. Buzz placed the fish in his trading bag and, with a deep, long sniff to stave off his craving, turned towards the fence. Looking left and right to check for patrolling sentries, he crouched low, ready to dash.

"Wrong side of the fence, Buzz!" A low deep purr right behind him made him leap sideways, dropping his bag. It was Kitty, a runaway she-cat. She snatched the bag and ran back towards Trade Point Wall.

"I need a trade today," she laughed. Buzz was quick to take her down before she got too close.

"Ouch! You're hurting me!" she cried as he pinned her into the grassy sand, grabbing his bag. Still against the palisade and not the wall, Buzz was aware that they were easy targets.

"Who goes there?" a deep voice called. It was the sentry patrolling the boundary fence.

Buzz and Kitty looked at one another and held completely still, their bodies lying flat in the grass.

"I said who goes there?" came the voice again. "Show yourselves, or there will be trouble."

"It's only me!" came Tikana's voice from the other side of the fence. The hair on Buzz's back stood up, and he dug his nails into the bag.

"And what are you doing down here so close to the fence?" the sentry huffed. "The fence is out of bounds during trading!"

"I'm sorry. I must have wandered without thinking. I'll be off then," she replied, turning to leave.

"If you are caught here again, there will be a penalty from the prince himself!" insisted the sentry.

Tikana's whiskers twitched, and she went trotting through the grass. The sentry marched off back towards Trade Point Wall.

When the coast was clear, Kitty dashed to the fence to try to get a look at Tikana. There was no one to be seen.

"Odd! Now that was extremely coincidental. Almost felt like she was watching and came to help us out," Kitty mused.

Buzz ignored her and dashed through the fence.

"Well, tell your girlfriend I say hello!" Kitty called after him. Buzz stopped dead and turned around. He glared at Kitty and then disappeared into the undergrowth.

uzz flew through the bushes, all the time sniffing for Tikana. A good distance from the trading, he stopped and mewed. He knew that the risk he'd taken today was too high.

"I'm here, Buzz." Tikana's whisper came floating down with some leaves. Buzz looked up into the tall trees above him. He was not too keen on climbing up and motioned with his head for her to come down. Buzz was dreading her lecture. She eased her way down the tree and stood in front of him. Their eyes met, and Buzz looked down. He picked up his bag and started walking. Tikana didn't move. "It's a pleasure!" she called after him. He stopped and looked back.

"So it didn't go as I had planned. I'm sorry you got caught in the middle of it."

"In the middle of it? Buzz, I came to your rescue," mewed Tikana.

There was a long pause. Buzz flicked the air with his tail. "I was completely in control of the situation."

"No, you weren't!" argued Tikana. "You were moments from—"

"Making my own plan to get out!" snapped Buzz.

"What is it with you? Tikana mewed. "Or am I the problem? I just can't ever do anything right in anyone's eyes!"

"Don't say that about yourself," spat Buzz. "I've watched how you have changed over the past few weeks. You're one of the most fearless cats I know."

"Fearless and friendless," Tikana spat back.

"Truth is not always popular. I'm sorry about today, and thank you for what you did just now. It could have gone really badly." Buzz looked back towards the fence. "Come on. I've got a surprise for you tonight."

* * *

Tikana didn't really like the inside of Buzz's den. It was earthy and damp, hidden behind one of the benches on the estate. Buzz was a collector of all kinds of things, and the back of the den was a treasure trove of trinkets. Tikana sniffed through them while Buzz prepared the river fish. She had never had river fish before and was quite nervous.

There was a knock at the entrance to the den. Tikana stiffened as she smelt wild cat.

"Who goes there?" called Buzz.

"One who wishes to dine with friends," came the reply.

Tikana's eyes lit up as she recognized Asti's voice. She rushed to the entrance and rubbed her face in Asti's neck.

"Look at you!" purred Asti. "Regal and bright! Tafari won't—"

Buzz coughed and interrupted her. "Dinner is served!"

Asti gave him a questioning glance and then spotted the evening's fare. "River fish pie!" she exclaimed. "Only domestic cats seem to be able to make it like this!" She took a long, deep breath.

Tikana tentatively licked around the edge of her plate. The thought of eating wild fish caught by wild cats was quite a lot to stomach. Her first few mouthfuls were unfamiliar, but then something delightful filled her whole being. She looked up at Buzz and Asti smiling at her and realized it was the first time she had ever eaten with friends. Her fur stood to attention, and her whiskers tingled. Warmth filled her up, and the pie tasted out of this world!

They laughed and spoke deep into the early hours of the morning until at last it was time for Asti to leave.

"Before you leave," questioned Tikana tentatively, "is there any news of Tafari?"

Buzz flashed a look at Asti before she turned towards Tikana and smiled. "He has gone far up river to talk to the princes of the Eastern River Lands. It has not been two moons since. Keep your heart still while you wait."

"It's just that the longer I wait, the more I wonder..." mewed Tikana.

"The more you wonder whether you are in love with the reality of Tafari or the mystery," hushed Asti.

Tikana shut her eyes tight. She had never spoken of her love for Tafari to anyone.

"You must have patience in this, beautiful one. Don't be ashamed of your feelings. Even if nothing comes of them, treasure them. It means you are alive!" Asti had a twinkle in her eye as she swept out of the den, closely followed by Buzz. As soon as they were out of Tikana's earshot, Buzz leaned over to Asti.

"The toms are calling for a statue. It's never going to happen. She is so full of hope."

"If Tikana is his soul mate, a path will open up for them, with or without a statue," Asti purred. "Now go back and be her friend. Your open heart is healing her."

"Well, I did almost get her arrested today," mumbled Buzz, but it was into the blackness. Asti had already disappeared.

CHAPTER THIRTY

The moon was almost full, and Buzz had a feeling it was his last chance to help Tikana before the return of the prince. He would wait until the stars started to fade and morning appeared on the horizon. Wild cats always threw parties at the river on nights when the moon was bright. Buzz knew that he had a couple of hours to go unnoticed. He would sneak down to the river under the cover of darkness and then carry out his plan while the wild cats slept in the first hours of light. He had been very preoccupied for the past couple of days and was sure that Tikana was suspicious. He knew he would have to be quick or he may not be back before she came looking for him in the morning.

Buzz waited for the river guards to pass and then, quick as a flash, made his way down through the fence. It was later than he had planned, and he could clearly see his way to the den. Hopefully most of the cats would be asleep by now.

ikana woke early. She had a feeling in the pit of her stomach that something was up. It was still dark, and she had promised Buzz not to leave her apartment until he was there. She looked out of the window. There was no one around, and although the fountain was still floodlit, the stars were beginning to fade. Tikana slipped outside. The air was fresh and still. Dashing across the courtyard, she made her way to Buzz's favourite night perch, sure he would be there, all ready to give her a lecture about coming to find him. As Tikana approached the bench that concealed Buzz's hidden den, she noticed a piece of metal shining in the moonlight. She picked it up and inspected it. It was the zip from Buzz's trading bag. Curious, she thought. Buzz hadn't traded since the incident at the fence. She slipped behind the bench and through the ivy into the den.

"Buzz?" she called. Silence. The den was dark and empty. Tikana lit a candle.

Strewn over the floor were bits of rope, bottles, and wood, and taped carefully onto the wall was a drawing. It was a rough sketch of a raft. Tikana felt like she was spying, but curiosity got the better of her, and she started to flick through the pieces of paper on his desk. There were a couple of letters he had started to Tafari, but he had never gotten past "To his Royal Highness the Prince..."

There was nothing very interesting that caught her eye, and Tikana made her way back towards the entrance, tripping on a piece of crumpled paper on her way. She unfurled it and held it up to the light. It was a drawing of Jethro's den, the river, and the trees. There were arrows here and there pointing towards the river and illegible notes around the edge.

How strange, she thought. Buzz must be up to something.

Tikana deliberated for a while and then decided to try to find Asti. She was always up for an adventure.

CHAPTER THIRTY TWO

The old oak was silent with shadows, and the fur along her spine stood up. She called out a couple of times, but there was no answer. Asti was nowhere. Tikana would have to investigate alone. The willow tree branches pulled her out of the oak tree and over the fence. Staying up high, she made her way towards Jethro's old den.

Tikana knew that she was vulnerable all alone in the River Lands, but she felt unusually free, almost wild. Somehow the earth smelt richer and the fragrances from the indigenous trees headier than inside the complex. The dawn light stretched through the leaves, making everything grey before turning yellow. She wasn't quite sure of the way but knew that if she kept the fence on her right and the river on her left, she would find it.

A couple of times she came around a bend only to find herself directly in front of the river with nowhere to pass, and once she almost walked straight into the fence. After what seemed like an age, something about the smell set her pulse racing, and she climbed up high to try to get a good overview.

There, down below her, was the sandy patch, the entrance to the den. And there was Buzz, in the middle of the river, balancing on what looked like some kind of raft! Quick as a flash, Tikana sped down the tree. The river by the den was fast flowing—not like the evening of the storm when they were all held prisoner by Jethro but still too strong to swim across.

Buzz was standing on the raft, which was secured with rope on both banks of the river. To a willow tree on the far side and to a huge rock next to the den. Tied to an overhanging branch, Buzz had a large net in his paws with which he was scooping up sand and pebbles. He carefully sorted through them before throwing them back over the other side of the raft.

"Buzz!" called Tikana over the river. "What on earth are you doing?"

Buzz got such a fright when he looked up and saw her that he lost his footing, sending the raft shooting out behind him. He was held suspended over the river for a few moments until the raft came back underneath him. He looked frustrated and angry.

"What are you doing here, Tikana? It's far too dangerous for you!"

"I should ask you the same question. Did you think I was going to sleep all morning? Everyone keeps saying it's far too dangerous all the time. What actually is the danger? Jake is dead, and Jethro is gone, so I don't really see what you are all so worried about!" Tikana flicked her tail and turned away.

"Wild cats are not like us, and they certainly are not all like Asti. You are a she-cat, and you are royalty." And he added under his breath, "Royalty without proof!"

"Right now I wish I could just be the old Tikana with no pretend friends and no royal blood!"

Buzz rolled his eyes. "Go home, Tikana!" He pointed to a large thorn tree sticking out above the trees. "That thorn tree is at the fence. Titanic will be on guard. Wait there with him until I come for you."

Tikana glared at him and then obeyed. She climbed back up into the trees and hid in the branches where she could watch from a distance. Buzz continued his search, being swept this way and that by the current, pulling out pile after pile of stones and sand. Tikana could see that he was growing more and more frustrated, and in a flash she knew what he was doing.

He was trying to find the golden statue!

"You'll never change," she snarled under her breath. "Once a trader, always a trader!" All the old feelings of mistrust came flooding back. "Sneaking off to steal my statue. I suppose he thinks he can trade it for a fortune!" she blurted out to herself. She was angry now and flicked back towards the fence. She had seen enough.

Tikana had almost reached the thorn tree when she heard a giant crack. The sound came from the direction of the den. She braced, digging her claws into the bark. Two voices in her head argued with each other—one determined to keep going, angry with Buzz, and the other urging her to go back and help. Reluctantly she turned around and then took up speed.

The branch holding Buzz had snapped and fallen into the river. It was caught on the bank, the other end bouncing wildly in the water. Buzz had been pulled off his raft and was frantically swimming upstream, trying to reach the branch, still tied to the rope.

Like lightning, Tikana was on the bank next to the den. She wedged two stones under the branch to try to keep it stable and then carefully crept out over the river, digging her claws into the wet wood. Buzz was starting to tire, and the current kept sweeping him under water. Reaching the rope, Tikana pulled and pulled, but Buzz was really too heavy for her. With the branch bouncing so wildly, Tikana started to lose her grip. A sudden jerk caused one of the rocks to roll down the bank, and the branch became even more unstable. Tikana closed her eyes. She was barely holding on.

"Tikana!" yelled Buzz. "Untie the rope and get off the branch. It's going to roll!"

Tikana tried, but the knot was under the water and too tight for her. Suddenly she had an idea. She leapt onto the raft, which was calmly floating a small distance from the bank. Carefully she climbed up the rope and onto the willow tree on the other side of the river. Moving along one of the overhanging branches, she used her weight to tip the ends of the thin branches into the water.

"Buzz! Over here," she called, and he started to swim across, which was slightly easier than straight upstream. The water was a lot calmer where the willow hung over the river. Tikana needed to crawl out a little further along the branch, as only the tips were in the water and not enough for Buzz to grab onto. Cautiously she crouched low and edged out further. Buzz was almost at the branches when he realized that the rope around his waist was not long enough. He tried to untie the rope as he treaded water.

"Quickly!" urged Tikana. "The rocks are slipping!"

Buzz took a breath and, using his teeth underwater, managed to untie the cord. He was just in time to watch the entire branch slip down into the river and pick up speed as it floated down stream, the rope still attached. With a leap for the willows, Buzz was up and out of the water, but Tikana was too far out, and the weight of the two cats on the thin branches caused them to start pulling out of the trunk. The cats were violently swung towards the trunk and jerked back up into the air before crashing down into the water.

Gasping for air, Tikana screamed for help and tried to scramble back up the leafy strands, Buzz following her.

All the while the tearing branches were ripping away from the tree, and the cats were getting lower and lower, both of them now in the water.

"Buzz, Tikana, up here!" It was Titanic. He was straddled between two overhanging branches, moving them towards the cats like rescue ropes.

"Grab on!" exclaimed Titanic, and he swung the branches low and over their heads. The cats leapt for the branches. They were safe at last.

Shivering and scared to death, Tikana led the way back over to the raft and along the second rope onto the rocks.

The sun was quite high now and felt warm and comforting.

"Are you all right, Your Majesty?" asked Titanic.

"Yes," Tikana replied, out of breath.

She looked at Buzz, still angry with him for being mean.

Buzz looked down, embarrassed and feeling like a failure. Not only had he not found the statue, but Tikana, with the help of Titanic, had saved his life. He was meant to be the bodyguard!

"I'm sorry, Tikana," he said softly. "I've failed you." And he walked slowly into the trees and disappeared.

"Buzz!" Tikana called after him. "Wait!" But she was too tired to run; her front legs ached, and her body was shivering out of control.

Titanic felt uneasy standing alone with Tikana down at the river. He was not her appointed bodyguard, and if any of the toms saw him, they would accuse her of trying to gain favour with the council. Even worse, if Tafari saw them, Buzz would be banished for abandoning his charge, and Tafari may think he was trying to make advances on his princess.

"Your Majesty...." He hesitated. "We must get back to the fence. Can you try to walk?"

"Buzz!" Titanic pleaded again, hoping he could get Buzz back. "Please, Your Majesty. You must get up!"

Tikana murmured and lifted her head. "Can't we just rest a few minutes, please, Titanic?"

"Well, all right," he answered, "but I shall keep watch from up in the trees. You start walking when you are ready."

Tikana closed her eyes. She had always been petrified of water and was so grateful to feel the dry earth under her wet body.

She was soon fast asleep.

uzz was feeling foul. He had failed the prince, and although he had never aspired to be a bodyguard, he had rather enjoyed his new role.

"Useless, patchy furball!" Buzz could hear the voice of his father from when he was young. His father had been a sentry and always wanted Buzz to become one. But Buzz was after freedom and loved exploring down at the river. That was how he became a trader, something his father always disapproved of.

Not looking where he was going and quite wrapped up in failures, Buzz walked straight into Tafari.

"Your Majesty," Buzz gasped.

Tafari's face lit up, and immediately he looked into the bushes from where Buzz had come, but there was no one behind him. Tafari's searching eyes made Buzz look down.

"Where is Tikana?" asked Tafari calmly. "Is she not well that she has stayed in her apartment today? Why are you limping and wet?"

Buzz felt a large bead of sweat drop from his forehead. How could he answer Tafari now? Hanging his head, all he could muster was, "Banish me. I have failed you."

"What?" cried Tafari. "Where is she?"

Buzz pointed in the direction of the den. Tafari was gone before Buzz could even explain.

ell, well, well," mocked Magnum, "if it isn't the princess!"

Tikana was woken from her sleep. She hadn't been asleep for long, but her hair had dried on the one side, and on standing she realized that she was covered with mud and a couple of leaves had stuck to the side of her face.

"Not the beautiful golden princess now, are you?" continued Magnum, who had come across her on his morning stroll at the river. "In fact, you don't even have proof of your nobility." His voice was sarcastic and mean. "Covered in mud and leaves, and you call yourself a princess?"

"No," insisted Tikana. "I have never called myself a princess. It was you and Buzz and everyone else who called me princess!"

"And Tafari? What does he call you? You know he will never take you as his bride without proof."

Tikana gaped.

"No words, Your Majesty? Or should I repeat myself?" Magnum was so close, Tikana could feel his breath in her ear when he hissed, "Tafari will take no princess without a statue!" He glared at her, and she was shocked into silence by his cruelty.

"And what else won't I do?" boomed Tafari as he landed on the ground behind Magnum.

Turning around, Magnum smiled at Tafari. "I was just wondering what the princess was doing covered in mud and leaves, down at the river, alone!"

"She is not alone," interrupted Titanic, jumping down from the tree. "Your Majesty, may I explain?"

While everyone was looking at Titanic, Tikana quickly brushed the leaves from her face and tried to remove the mud with a wet paw.

Tafari raised his paw. He ignored Magnum for the moment and walked over to Tikana, touching her cheek. "Are you all right?" he asked.

Tafari seemed different to Tikana. There was a warmth around him, almost as though she could see deeper into his eyes for the first time. He had always seemed quite distant and aloof.

"Tikana, are you all right?" he asked again, this time looking down at the river and noticing the raft.

"Yes, Tafari—I mean, Your Majesty. I am alive, thank you."

Her heart had started to beat rapidly, and Tikana wondered why she hadn't just said, "Fine, thank you." Whenever Tafari was around she used such awkward words.

Tafari just smiled and pointed towards the raft. "Is that Buzz's boat?" he asked.

"Yes," answered Titanic. "They were...um, well...I am not sure what they were doing, but when I found them, Tikana was attempting to rescue Buzz across the river."

"But Titanic ended up rescuing us all!" interrupted Tikana.

"Tikana rescuing someone? Pah!" smirked Magnum. "She wouldn't know how to do that. Probably can't even swim. All Tikana is good for is interrupting meetings and standing up for pathetic little kittens! She is an embarrassment of a princess!"

Tafari stood absolutely still, every muscle in his body tensed and ready to pounce on Magnum, when out of the bushes appeared Buzz.

"Not an embarrassment, Magnum," said Buzz. "The truth is she embarrassed you by standing up for what was right at the quarter season assembly, and today she embarrassed me by attempting to save my life. She is not the embarrassment. We are. I was meant to be protecting her, and yet she was the one who rescued me from almost drowning."

"What were you doing, Buzz?" asked Tafari.

"Well, if you must know, I was looking for the golden statue."

Tikana gasped. She was right all along. "How could you, Buzz? That statue is not to be traded and sold. It belongs to the royal families."

"I know," said Buzz, hurt filling his eyes. "That was why I was trying to recover it—as your proof."

Tikana's eyes went wide. "You were doing that for me? Why?"

"So Tafari can take you as his bride!" interjected Magnum. "It is his wish, but there will be no bride without proof!"

Tikana felt every hair on her body flatten, and she had no idea where to look. So Tafari did think she was beautiful, and he did intend to tell her. Wishing he had told her first, her embarrassment quickly turned into disappointment. How she longed to disappear into the trees! Without proof, did he also doubt her royalty? Her legs felt like pins and needles as the life quickly drained out of her.

Tafari looked at Tikana, wishing she wasn't there. He had wanted to tell her for himself about how he felt and explain everything when the time was right. He could see how uncomfortable she was, and he desperately wanted her to like him. He never wanted it to be like this. He had planned to take her for long walks and down to the river to dance with the wild cats before revealing his intent.

He had first seen her a year before at one of the meetings and had been captivated by her beauty, but his wounded heart and her missing statue had kept him from pursuing her. Instead he had watched her from a distance, always remaining hidden, feeling powerless to set her free from the lies, his heart breaking from her pain. Then, when she had suddenly appeared back in his life on that fateful night, he knew she was his destiny. He was willing to risk everything for her love. But he also knew that she would need to see his heart, to understand and love him as a friend. More than that, she would need to believe the truth about who she really was, even without proof.

Tafari felt like pinning Magnum to the ground and pounding him until he was silent, but he remained steady, his muscles and his tail twitching.

"Tikana needs proof before the council," continued Magnum. "That is the law, Tafari, and you know it! All the toms are in agreement."

Tafari looked at Titanic. "You as well, my friend?"

"No. I told them that what they were speaking was treason. How long have we been friends, Tafari? Please don't doubt my faithfulness!"

"Has the council been meeting behind my back?" Tafari was enraged now, and Tikana crouched down low and turned her face away.

"How dare they!" roared Tafari.

"Your Majesty," pleaded Magnum, his tone sly and purring, "it was not an official meeting, just the end of a card game. We were all talking when someone mentioned the missing statue, and of course there is the problem of your brother

Jethro down in the storm water drains." Magnum lowered his tone. "You know the consequences of taking a bride without proof. Even if Buzz here were to have found that statue, who is to say where it came from in the first place? Each princess should have her own statue, given to her by her parents."

"Curse those statues, Magnum!" cried Tafari. "More bloodshed and tears are spilt over them than anything else in the kingdom. Tikana only doubts her royalty because cats like you place so much value on pieces of gold! You trust what you can see and touch over your heart's whisper. Everyone can see that Tikana is royalty. I myself have seen that statue and know it's hers! In fact, many of the council knew her mother Miltaka and her father Alnitak. Tikana has a noble heart, and it is her heart that I am in love with, not her statue."

There. He had said it; not to her but into the strained atmosphere.

"I have watched as Tikana has been mocked, teased, and rejected. I knew you would demand proof, so I waited, hoping it would appear, and when it did, who got hold of it? My brother, Jethro. I will not go against my heart anymore."

Tafari turned towards Tikana and lifted her tearful face to his.

"Tikana, I do not need to see proof. I am in love with you, not your title or bloodline. Your heart is as golden as your coat. You may not love me now, but please give me a chance to show you my heart."

"Oh, Tafari," burst out Tikana, "I do love you, beyond what I see with my eyes."

"Don't be a fool, Tafari!" insisted Magnum, ignoring the holiness of the moment. "You are just infatuated and captivated by her beauty. She must have a statue. Don't be naive about this. Jethro is a real threat to our peace, and so help me God I will not let you marry a royal question mark. Having two statues is the only way to break Jethro's claim to the throne. This is not about your heart and happiness but the kingdom's peace."

"Peace has not come to the River Lands through statues, Magnum, but through honour and love," said Tafari. "Even some of the dark lords have statues. Their statues empower their darkness. I will take Tikana as my bride when she is ready, statue or no statue."

"Then I shall say only one last thing. Tikana herself will admit that she is unsure of her bloodline. Spending days as the butt of people's jokes and being mocked and picked on for years has made her doubt, even to the point that she had no idea she was royal until a few weeks ago. The cats will not accept her without proof. Then you will have put her in a place of prominence for even more rejection and shame. Think carefully, my lord."

And with that, Magnum bowed and walked away into the bushes.

"He's right," sighed Tikana. "I am a joke."

"No, you're not!" said Buzz firmly. "Don't listen to Magnum. He is just jealous of Tafari. It's obvious."

"Hush now," said Tafari. "Tonight's full moon meeting will be at the Golden Pools for all cats, wild and domestic. Titanic, spread the news, and then meet me at my den."

"Tikana, I will make good on what I have vowed. What I have spoken today is the truth, and I will make the kingdom a safe place for you. The cats will love and respect you in time. Your heart will win them over, just as it has won me. Now go and find Asti. Buzz, keep her in your sight until this evening."

Tafari lifted his paw to reach out and touch Tikana's but hesitated at the last moment, suddenly unsure. Perhaps Magnum was right. Perhaps his selfish longing for Tikana would become such pain for her. He must think things through before tonight.

Tikana immediately felt his hesitation, and her heart reeled.

As they parted, Tikana and Tafari looked back at each other, having drawn veils over their hearts.

CHAPTER THIRTY FIVE

B y the time Tikana had found Asti, her heart felt like it was falling out. It was all too much for her.

"When we hope," whispered Asti, nudging Tikana's cheek, "we keep breathing. But when hope is lost, our hearts become sick, and we forget to breathe properly. I know exactly the right medicine for you!"

Asti leaped up and beckoned the others to follow. As they got to the fence, Asti whispered something in Buzz's ear, and he sped off up the garden inside the complex.

"You know, Tikana, your mother never intended it to be like this, but domestic cats have to make a choice when their owners move. She wanted to stay close to you. In fact, she was desperate, knowing that your father was dwelling beyond reach."

"Oh, tell me about my mother, Miltaka the Graceful," pleaded Tikana.

"Well," began Asti, "your mother and father ruled the glades for many years. But just after you were born, your father became ill, as you know." For a moment Asti paused, remembering their conversation in the big oak, and then continued. "He very quickly passed on to the unreachable spaces between the stars. Your mother was never quite the same after that. Her desire to rule was gone. Tafari and Jethro from the Western River Lands were next in line to the throne, as you were just a tiny baby and it was time for a new bloodline to reign. Jethro had no statue, so the crown fell to Tafari. Many of the older toms thought he was too young, but it was the beginning of a new era. Wild and tame cats ruled by the same prince, loved by the same prince, served by the same prince.

"Your mother mourned your father so deeply she almost lost her life. That was when they took you away from her and gave you as a gift to their neighbour. To save her life. You were the smallest kitten on the estate, a bit like PC. No mother to guide you or teach you. She wept for you but had to leave with her owners. She would never have made it in the wild."

"I wept too and have longed for her return," said Tikana. "When the other cats started to tease me, I had no one to talk to and no friends. Even Buzz was nasty to me. It broke my heart, and I vowed that I would never be like that to other cats, no matter what they did to me."

"Your mother would be so proud of you, Tikana. I know she regrets every day she hasn't been able to be with you."

"Do you think I will ever see her again?" asked Tikana.

"Sometimes I can see your destiny, but I can't see your future. Most certainly you will be with her one day, in the spaces between the stars."

"Tikana! Tikana!"

It was PC. Buzz had gone to fetch him on Asti's orders. He flung his paws around Tikana and nuzzled his face in her fur.

"I love you so much!" he said.

"And I love you too, little one," said Tikana, laughing.

Then PC spoke and spoke and spoke, asking questions and telling stories of all his adventures around the estate. He made Tikana smile and play chase with him, and the day passed quickly.

As the shadows were getting longer, PC said good-bye and went home. He had been the perfect medicine for Tikana, making her promise to play with him more.

Buzz had been quiet all afternoon. His mind could not be distracted, and a heaviness had come over him. What would happen at the meeting? There had never been a meeting of wild and tame cats together, with only a palisade fence separating them.

The Golden Pools was a section of the river right next to the fence. A giant boulder ran right through the boundary line and could not be removed by the builders, so the fence ran straight across the top of it. It was quite a wild and hidden part of the estate, and the river often got caught in the rocks when it flooded, creating pools that shone like gold in the sunset.

As Tikana, Buzz, and Asti approached the pools they were indeed golden. The three sat, their eyes reflecting the sunset in silence, until cats started arriving for the meeting. Asti nodded to Tikana before slipping under the fence and sitting right against it on top of the rock.

CHAPTER THIRTY SIX

There was a strange silence that night, with wild and tame eyeing each other through the fence, perched on either side of the boulder. Tikana stayed mostly hidden from view in the shadows between two rocks, Buzz perched just above her. Even the sentries were quiet and spoke to each other in hushed tones. There were no clouds, and the stars were out until the moon rose, rubbing out their glory. Waiting for their prince, the cats were entranced in the moonlight. Howling dogs and distant sirens were all that could be heard.

Titanic at last stepped forward and stood at the top of the rock on the estate side of the fence. "His Majesty, the Prince!" he cried, and the cats from the estate bowed down low. Then, slipping through the fence, he repeated it to the wild cats on the river side. They too bowed down. And while everyone was bowing, Tafari approached and sat down at the top of the rock. A murmur went through the crowd as they looked up. He was truly majestic, his fur glistening in the moonlight and his eyes shining.

"Cats of the River Kingdom, I come before you tonight with one request, that you will hear my heart and be slow to judge. There are some of you who are indeed old enough to remember the reign of Alnitak the Fearless and Miltaka the Graceful."

Many of the cats bowed their heads in remembrance of their great leaders.

"Tonight should be a time of great rejoicing as I announce my chosen bride, daughter of these two great leaders: Tikana, Princess of the Southern Cross." The crowd gasped and then murmured, their whispers getting louder and louder.

Tafari raised his paw, and silence fell once again.

"I realize that this comes as a great surprise to many of you. The object of your scorn is indeed what you always called her—a princess."

"We need proof!" the crowd clamoured. "Where is her statue?"

The sentinels spread out amongst the crowd keeping watch for troublemakers.

"Tikana had no mother," came a voice from the crowd. "I knew Miltaka and remember her well. She never had any daughters! Tikana only came to the estate after she had left. Miltaka would never have abandoned her kitten!"

There were mutterings and murmurs arising from the crowd until cats started to bawl out, "We want proof! We want proof!" The sound from the writhing, dangerous crowd rose way above the river.

On the river side, the crowd was quiet, still afraid of life in the estate and suspicious of the tame. They knew nothing of Tikana and had never even seen her. Their curiosity silenced them as they waited for the prince to continue. With a raised paw, he silenced the estate.

"Miltaka left when Tikana was only a few weeks old, too sick with grief to look after her following Alnitak's death. Tikana herself has only faint memories of her mother. But I ask you this. Can a statue breathe and speak? Does it tell of a person's heart? Does it have eyes to see what the very cat it represents is doing? I have a statue, given to me by my father. Does this statue tell me what to do in the morning? Do I ask for its opinion? Does it shape my heart? Many of the dark lords of the river crossing have statues. Do those statues make them noble or just empower their darkness?"

The crowd had fallen silent now, feeling the depth of what Tafari was saying, even though many of them were not able to understand as yet. Although they were listening, they could not hear beyond their ears.

"I am not in love with a statue but a live, breathing, hearing, talking heart. Tikana's heart. With which of you has she ever fought back and made low with her words? Tikana has only given grace to you whilst her heart has broken from your cruelty. I have watched as she selflessly put her life on the line for a kitten and bravely fought off two of the meanest wild cats in the River Lands. She has embraced and loved one of her worst antagonists and welcomed the wild cats into her heart. This is my choice, and I ask that you will search your hearts tonight and make a decision not based on a statue but based on who Tikana, Princess of the Southern Cross, really is."

Tikana was crouched down so low that Buzz couldn't even see her. Her whole body was a tightly wound ball of muscle. Her prince had taken her side, risking everything for her love. She could hardly breathe, crouched between those two rocks, and her body was numb in its quivering.

Some of the cats had walked away in disgust, spitting on the ground as they pushed through the crowd. But mostly they looked down, ashamed of what was in their hearts.

Hissing softly in approval of their proposed princess, the wild cats kept their heads up, wanting to catch their first view of her.

It was an old retired sentry who broke the silence. "Long live Princess Tikana! Long live Prince Tafari!"

The crowd hesitated. Then a few voices joined in, soon rising to many.

"Long live Princess Tikana! Long live Prince Tafari!"

Tikana felt at peace. She lifted up her head, albeit still in the shadows. The crowd was cheering for her—even Magnum, who was now standing next to Tafari. He raised his paw to speak. Tikana's heart sank; would this now be the end for her?

"Cats of the River Lands," he began, "I too have spoken wrongly of Tikana and treated her harshly. Only today did I come to my senses, and I have sought forgiveness of the prince. Tikana, wherever you are—and I know you are indeed here..." The crowd looked around everywhere, and Magnum paused. "For a while I could not see, and I am sorry. I ask your forgiveness for placing so much trust in a piece of gold that I could not trust my own heart. Or indeed the discernment of my faithful prince and his heart."

The night held so still for that moment. Tikana looked up at Buzz, and he bowed his head. Courage held her and caused her legs to stretch and move up out of her hiding place. As soon as Tafari caught a glimpse of her, he ran down and pressed his face up against her. Their tails flicked and touched. Together they walked up boundary rock, Tikana shining a golden bronze in the moonlight. A great cheer went up from the crowd.

Tafari raised his paw once more and with great softness said, "Thank you." Then over a great roar, he said, "I present to you my chosen bride, Tikana, Princess of the Southern Cross, daughter of Alnitak the Fearless and Miltaka the Graceful."

With that the crowd bowed low and then purred and hissed with excitement. The wild cats did the same, as Tafari led Tikana through the fence.

There was nothing left but great revelry and excitement at the thought of the coming festivities. Full of joy and praise for Tafari's choice and his deep love for Tikana, the cats retreated to their homes.

CHAPTER THIRTY SEVEN

The sentinels moved to position themselves, protecting the small group on top of boundary rock. Tikana turned to her beloved Tafari. She came right up close, bowed low and then placed her head on his chest.

"I am yours, Tafari," she said. "Thank you for believing in me, for seeing my heart. For not needing proof. Today you have indeed set all cats free to become noble in their hearts."

Tafari held her head tightly to his chest.

Buzz coughed a few times and cleared his throat before speaking. "I have been honoured to be your bodyguard, Tikana, but now, Your Majesty, may I be relieved of my duties and hand her over to Titanic?"

Tafari laughed. "Buzz, I am so proud of you. May I call you friend?"

Buzz looked down sheepishly. Then, grinning, he said, "Yes, Your Majesty." Then he turned to Tikana. "I am so sorry I couldn't find your statue. I have been so honoured to walk this journey with you, and I promise never again to eat your breakfast!" He said this with a wink, and everyone laughed.

Tafari nodded his head at Buzz, deep gratitude in his eyes.

Titanic stepped up to the top of the rock. "Your Majesty, I have waited for so long to accept the honour of protecting your bride."

Tafari patted him on the back, and they laughed. "Guard her with your life, Titanic, my faithful friend."

Titanic turned towards Tikana and bowed low.

"Thank you, Titanic. You believed in me even when there was so much doubt."

"I knew your father," he said in almost a whisper. "You have the same markings, on the outside and the inside."

Tikana's eyes welled up with tears, and she looked up into the sky. She then turned her face towards Magnum, humbled and quizzical. He saw that she was struggling to accept his sudden change of heart and looked at Tafari. The prince nodded as if to give him space to explain himself.

"Your Majesty," began Magnum, "pride can be such an enormous wall, and one over which I have had to climb, even today. I was indeed embarrassed by the turn of events at the quarter season assembly, and yes, you were right. The way I treated PC was unforgivable. I lost the affection of a beautiful she-cat through that, and it has fuelled my anger towards you—unjustly. But when Tafari challenged me at the river this morning, it was as though I suddenly felt so shallow.

I could not trust my heart without a piece of gold. I wrestled and toiled for hours, not knowing what to do.

"I wandered down to the river and saw Buzz's raft still floating there. I jumped onto it and lay quite still, feeling the water rocking to and fro. I leaned my head over the side to get more comfortable and was suddenly blinded by a flash."

The cats all leaned in towards Magnum, not quite believing what they were hearing. He continued, "I went back onto the shore and grabbed the net. Carefully, lying quite far out on the raft, I scanned the water again and waited for the same flash. As soon as I was sure of the exact location, I dipped the net in and scooped. Up came a mound of stones and sand." Magnum paused, reached into his pocket. "And this statue, pure, shining gold."

The cats all gasped in surprise and awe.

"What the heck!" cried Buzz. "You had her statue all along and didn't say anything!"

"Keep your voices low," urged Tafari, looking at Magnum in disbelief.

"Please let me explain my secrecy. My first thought was to rush and tell you, but then I knew what to do." Magnum took Tikana's paw in his. "Tonight the cats accepted you forever without a statue, not because they could see a gold replica of you but because they saw your heart and believed in you. After everything I put you through, I wanted you to be accepted without a statue, that you may forever believe the truth about yourself, not because there is a statue but because we all saw your heart.

I had the statue ready to pull out if things got bad, but they didn't, and so here, Your Majesty, is your golden statue." He held the statue out to Tikana.

Tafari stepped forwards and pushed Magnum's paw aside. "You did the right thing, Magnum. Now go and bury it, making sure no one sees you."

"No," broke in Asti. "Tikana must bury it, for truly it is hers, and only she must know where it lies. Tonight she has walked into her destiny without needing it, which will probably make her the most powerful princess ever to have ruled the River Lands." She looked at Tafari, a deep knowing between them.

"You are right," said Tafari.

Tikana held her statue, and a fear came over her. She realized what it must be like to be accepted only because of the gold in your hand. "I will bury it as soon as possible," she said. "I know just the place!" And she wrapped it quickly in some leaves.

The moon was very close to the horizon, and the morning star was hanging over the east.

"The night has come to an end," said Titanic. "It is time to depart."

Tafari looked disappointed but knew that he had a lifetime to get to know Tikana now that she had promised to be his.

She lifted her paw to Tafari's, and they glanced shyly into each other's eyes.

"Good night, my princess," said Tafari.

"Good night, my prince," she replied.

"Perhaps I should just escort Tikana home with Titanic," mumbled Buzz, feeling suddenly strange about letting her out of his sight. Everyone laughed, except Titanic, who took his job extremely seriously. He stepped in front of Buzz and ushered Tikana down the rock. Asti blew her a kiss, and she smiled back before turning and walking next to Titanic.

The small party on the rocks watched until they were out of sight.

Buzz stepped quietly through the bushes, holding the net between his teeth. The air was cool and clouds of mist arose from his breath. He crossed a large rock till down below him the silent pools swirled and mirrored his form. Putting down the net, he crept up close to the rim. Deep under the water lay his wind chime.

Made in the USA
Middletown, DE
10 January 2017